D0908254

RIDING WITH HANNAH AND THE HORSEMAN

RIDING WITH HANNAH AND THE HORSEMAN

•

Johnny D. Boggs

AVALON BOOKS
THOMAS BOUREGY AND COMPANY, INC.
401 LAFAYETTE STREET
NEW YORK, NEW YORK 10003

Library of Congress Catalog Card Number 98-96074
ISBN 0-8034-9300-2

PRINTED IN THE UNITED STATES OF AMERICA
ON ACID-FREE PAPER
BY HADDON CRAFTSMEN, BLOOMSBURG, PENNSYLVANIA

For Jack L. Smith,
my father-in-law,
and an all-around
epic character

Chapter One

Christmas came to the Davis Mountains on a false spring. The snow that had blanketed Sleeping Lion Mountain and Wild Rose Pass was long gone as the warm front settled in, and Hannah Scott decided to take advantage of it by asking Pete Belissari and Buddy Pecos to move the tables and chairs outside for Christmas supper. When the table was finally set, she went to check on the turkey in the cookshed behind the cabin.

The five orphan children that Hannah raised played with their toys near the corral, while Pete sweetened Buddy's coffee with a shot of ouzo.

"So what are your plans?" Belissari asked.

Pecos rubbed his forehead over the large brown leather patch that covered his right eye. He had served as acting sheriff of Presidio County since June before losing the November election to Tyler "Slick" Slaughter. Buddy hadn't done much campaigning—after the election he said, "Most folks I talked to said they'd vote for me, so I reckon Presidio County's just plumb full of liars"—but Pete suspected that the former Confederate sharpshooter really didn't want to be a lawman. He couldn't blame him for that.

And Slick Slaughter knew how to stump, befriending merchants and listening to ranchers, kissing babies and singing the praises of Texas and his kinfolk who had died at the Alamo.

"I'll figure somethin' out," Pecos said finally and sipped his coffee.

"Hannah bought a hundred head of cattle," Pete suggested. "We could always use some help around here. I'm not much of a cowman."

The aroma of stuffed turkey grabbed both men's attention as Hannah set the beautiful bird on the table. "I would have voted for you, Buddy," Hannah said, "if they'd let women vote."

"Maybe we should move to Wyoming," Pete said, picking up the carving knife. "Buddy could run for sheriff and Hannah could vote."

"How's that?" Pecos asked.

"Wyoming," Pete explained. "Women can vote in Wyoming."

Pecos's cold blue eye locked on Belissari for half a minute. "That," he said, "is the craziest thing I ever heard."

Belissari swallowed and ducked, half-expecting Hannah to hurl the bowl of mashed potatoes in Buddy's direction, but she only rolled her eyes and called for the children to wash up before supper.

"I been to Wyoming," Pecos said absently as he polished off his coffee. "Gets mighty cold up there. Reckon I'll stay in Texas."

After everyone was seated and Chris, the oldest of the children, had mumbled something that resembled grace, Hannah suggested that they sing one Christmas carol before eating. Pete's stomach grumbled, but he didn't protest. And when Hannah suggested that Pecos start a song, Belissari had to sit down, hold his breath, and squeeze the knife handle as hard as he could to keep from laughing.

"I ain't much for singin'," Pecos complained. "Don't reckon I know no Christmas tunes."

"Mr. Buddy," ten-year-old Angelica said, "everybody knows Christmas carols."

Pecos grunted and began to sing:

Oh, I'm a good old Rebel
Now that's just what I am
And for this Yankee nation
I do not give a—

"Buddy!" Hannah yelled. "That is not a Christmas carol!"

Pete exploded in laughter, knowing Hannah would make him pay dearly but unable to control himself. Cynthia jumped up and sang "Silent Night," saving Belissari and Pecos from being banned from the table, and the dinner proceeded without further incident. When the furniture was moved back inside, the dishes washed, the children put to bed, and Buddy Pecos seen off, Belissari stood by the corral that night, feeding sugar to his two prized horses, the mustang Duck Pegasus and the thoroughbred Lightning Flash. To his right, his gray saddle horse, Poseidon, snorted, lowered his head, and pawed the earth angrily with a forefoot.

"You'll get yours in a minute, boy," Pete said.

He felt Hannah beside him then, putting her arm around his waist for a few seconds, then reaching down and taking his left hand in her own and squeezing it gently. Her head rested against his shoulder and she said softly, ''Merry Christmas.''

''And to you.''

Belissari tossed the remaining cubes toward Poseidon and turned around, pulling her close and kissing her forehead. ''Not mad at Buddy and me anymore?''

''Don't worry,'' she said. ''You'll pay. You just don't know when.'' She sighed. ''What are we going to do about Buddy?''

''Buddy Pecos can take care of himself,'' he said. ''You don't need to worry about him.''

''Someone has to.''

Smiling, he reached into his pocket and pulled out a small box and placed it in her right hand. Her eyes widened and her mouth trembled. *Fright?* Pete wasn't sure. ''Don't worry,'' he said. ''It's not a ring.''

She opened the box and gasped. A gold necklace, with a ruby set in a beautiful star, glimmered in the moonlight. Pete had bought it at Sheilds Dry Goods in town, for a whopping thirteen dollars. The clerk swore that the woven necklace was solid gold, though the last time Pete bought gold jewelry for a woman, five years ago, a thin, green line had formed on his mother's wrist after wearing the bracelet for less than a day.

''You shouldn't have,'' Hannah said.

He only shrugged.

''I ordered you a pair of boots,'' she said apologetically as she slipped the necklace over her head. ''Buddy recommended this guy he knew in Spanish Fort on the Red River. I sent him a tracing of those Cordovan leather shoes I made you buy last summer. Anyway, they haven't arrived yet. Delivery's always slow out here. I'm sorry. I didn't want you to think I had forgotten you.''

Her eyes dropped toward the star necklace. ''It's beautiful, Pete. Thanks. Thank you so much—for everything.''

He kissed her. Poseidon snorted. Pete thought, *I hate wearing boots.* But when Hannah dropped the empty box and ran her fingers through his flowing hair, Pete Belissari forgot about cowboy boots and everything else in the world except Hannah Scott.

A week and a half later, Pete stood shaving in his cozy quarters next to the barn when the children screamed and he heard a strange commotion, causing him to nick his left cheek with the razor. He scratched the remaining beard stubble off his face and stepped outside, dabbing the cut with a wet bandanna, and stared, mouth open, at what Buddy Pecos rode into the yard.

Six ugly mules—one of them blind—were harnessed to a rickety, dilapidated old Concord stagecoach, the wheels squeaking and wobbly, peeling red paint faded to pink and caked with dust, the oil lamp on the right-hand side hanging upside down. In the driver's box sat Buddy Pecos, reins in his ungloved hands, and a bespectacled man wearing a linen duster over his sack suit and holding a brown bowler on his head with his left hand.

Pete tried to make out the company name painted over the stage's windows and doors but couldn't. He lifted the leather curtain and peaked inside. It was empty. That didn't surprise him. The floorboards appeared rotten, and he doubted if even a mouse would risk transportation in this old thing.

"Buddy," he said, stepping back and patting the neck of one of the tired mules. "What the Sam Hill are you doing?"

"Goin' into the stagecoachin' business with Mr. Everhart here."

The man lifted his hat and smiled.

"You paid money for this thing?"

"Six hundred dollars." Pecos spit a river of tobacco juice over the side. "Price includes the mules."

Pete shook his head. A brand new Wells Fargo and Company Overland Concord would cost maybe fifteen hundred dollars. Then again, an Overland stagecoach would likely get its passengers across Texas without falling apart.

"Buddy." It was Hannah. She smiled and put her hands on her hips. "You look dashing up there."

"I'm a regular jehu," he said. Pecos had done just about everything: soldier, cowboy, outlaw, buffalo hunter, bounty hunter, gunman, lawman, and now stagecoach driver, or as they liked to be called, a *jehu.*

"You and Pete hop aboard, and bring them young'uns. You'll be our first passengers. A free ride."

Smiling and shaking his head, Pete tied the bandanna around his neck, but the smile vanished as soon as Hannah said, "Really?" and the kids squealed in delight.

Pecos dropped from the box and opened the door. He pulled the folding step forward, but the device came off in his hand. Nonplussed, he tossed the rotten wood and rusted metal aside and swung Paco, Bruce, and Cynthia inside. Angelica and Chris followed, and then Hannah was grabbing Pete's arms and trying to pull him toward the wagon.

Pete's moccasins remained firmly rooted to the ground.

''Are you crazy?'' he asked.

Hannah chided him. ''Oh, come on, Petros. Don't be a fraidy cat.''

''Look at that thing.''

''It's not that bad. Get in. It got Buddy and this gentleman here without any problems I can see—''

''All the way from Fort Stockton, ma'am,'' Everhart added.

''And it's only ten miles to town,'' Hannah continued. ''Besides, maybe your boots have arrived, and I need some flour and coffee.''

Pete relented, against his better judgment. ''Not too fast, Buddy,'' Hannah said as the tall gunman rolled up the leather curtains before helping her inside.

''Don't worry, Miss Scott,'' Pecos said. ''Them mules is all tuckered out.''

Belissari ducked his head and pulled himself inside the Concord. It smelled of dust and odors he couldn't recognize—nor did he want to—but surprisingly the floor did not fall out underneath him. Four of the children sat in a seat behind the front boot, facing backward, and thirteen-year-old Chris stretched his lanky frame on the floor near the middle bench. Hannah, smiling like a schoolgirl, sat on the rear bench, and Pete found a spot beside her.

''Hiya! Hiya! Hiya! Get movin', mules!'' Pecos screamed as soon as he was back in his seat. A whip cracked. The stagecoach lurched forward. Pete Belissari felt his stomach turn over.

From Hannah Scott's ranch at the foot of Wild Rose Pass, the San Antonio–El Paso Road paralleled meandering Limpia Creek on a leisurely grade to the town of Fort Davis. The road had been part of the old Southern Overland Mail Route that John Butterfield had formed back in the late 1850s, and, for all Pete Belissari knew, this was one of Butterfield's original vehicles.

The problem with any stagecoach, Belissari thought, was with the carriage's suspension: a pair of thoroughbraces, strips of ox leather three inches thick. The coach rocked like an out-of-control cradle, and the passengers rolled—and often retched—with it.

Pete could ride just about anything. He had captured and broken mustangs for the Army and various ranches for years. At a Fourth of July gathering in the town of Pecos in 1883, he had ridden a sixteen-hand-high widow-maker stallion to a standstill, bareback. As the son of a ship's captain, he had been practically raised in the Gulf of Mexico, was used to gale winds, rough seas, even hurricanes. Truth was, he had never been seasick.

But traveling in a stagecoach was a different story. He closed his eyes, held his breath, and tried to keep his breakfast down his throat. The rear bench was the worst; the best seats were in the front, but he dared not move. He wondered if he would throw up into his hat. That would be embarrassing—in front of the kids, not to mention Hannah.

"Pete?" He felt Hannah's hand on his arm. "What's the matter?"

Refusing to open his eyes, he shook his head violently.

The stage hit a pothole. The thoroughbraces were supposed to absorb the shock, but the coach swayed wildly. Hannah laughed. The children cheered. Pete kicked a hole in the basswood panel.

He finally made himself open his eyes and glanced out the window to see the quartermaster corral at Fort Davis pass by in a flash, then the cavalry corrals, storehouses, and commissary office. *We're almost there,* he thought. *Hold on just a little more and we'll be in town.* He knew that he was pale, that the children were staring at him, but he didn't care.

At last, Buddy Pecos cried, "Whoa, you good-for-nothin' mules," and the unsettling Concord slowed down. Belissari pushed open the door and dived into the dusty street in front of Lightner's Saloon before the lathered mules had even come to a complete stop.

Chapter Two

The first thing he saw were the boots, gleaming black with cathedral arch stitching and no spurs. The first thing he heard was the laughter, booming rhythmically like a marksman spacing his shots. Pete Belissari rolled over, put his right arm over his forehead, and looked up at the ruddy face of Sheriff Slick Slaughter.

"Don't throw up on my boots, Peter my boy," Slaughter said. "I'd have to fine you for throwing garbage on my streets." He turned and stared at the old stagecoach, adding, "And there's enough garbage on these streets already."

Hannah knelt beside him, trying hard to hide her amusement, but failing. "You all right, Pete?"

"Yeah."

The world had stopped spinning, and he had choked back the bile in his throat. His stomach still felt a little queasy, the way it did when he was about to mount a widow-maker for the first time, but he was slowly regaining control. Slaughter's gray eyes, magnified behind his gold-rimmed spectacles, stared down at Pete again. He cracked another joke at Pete's expense, and the passersby who had gathered around laughed.

Slick Slaughter was a big man in his late fifties. The buttons on his gray vest strained to keep his sizable gut from popping out. He wore a black frock coat of fine wool, trimmed with red velvet, and black pants tucked inside his boots. His shirt was dark blue, partially covered by the coat, vest, and a black satin Claudent tie. A thick, gray mustache hid his upper lip and danced whenever he laughed or blinked. Sitting above his elephant ears and glasses was a wide-brimmed, open-crowned, mousy-colored hat. The catalogs called it nutria, and Pete found it fitting that Slaughter would choose that color. Nutria was the name of a big South American rodent.

Pete sat up, grabbed Buddy Pecos's proffered hand, and was yanked to his feet. Slaughter pulled back on his jacket, revealing his badge and hooking the tail behind his revolver, as if they didn't know he was the local law. "I hope you don't plan on leaving this junk on my streets too long," he told Pecos. "It'll give this town a bad name."

Pecos grunted something, and Slaughter laughed and walked off. Pete frowned. If anything had given Fort Davis a bad name, it was Slick Slaughter. The first thing he had done was revoke Buddy's ordinance prohibiting the carrying of firearms in the town limits. "It's bad for business," he told the Town Council. "We Texicans feel undressed without our six-guns." And business had improved for undertaker Hagen Schultz. Since December, he had buried two drunken cowboys—one who tried to kill a gambler, another who tripped over a cat while firing at the streetlights and accidentally shot himself—at Presidio County's expense.

"Need a drink?" Pecos asked.

"It wouldn't hurt," Pete replied.

Hannah smiled. "You men go ahead. I'll take the

children to the mercantile, then we might stop at the bakery. We'll meet you back here in a half hour or so."

Pete nodded, and Hannah, trailed by the five orphans, walked down the boardwalk.

"My bet's an hour," Pecos said.

"Hour and a half," Pete responded.

"I'm thirsty," said Everhart, whose presence had been forgotten by both men, and the three pushed through the batwing doors and into Lightner's Saloon.

Robert the bartender drew three beers and slid the mugs to the new customers. Pecos flipped a gold piece to the Cajun and waited for his change. The saloon was crowded for midmorning, and Pete turned and leaned against the bar, sipping on his beer, staring at a crowd around a poker table.

Ossian Philley, who ran a mercantile in Presidio, sat at the table, alternately eyeballing his cards and mopping his face with a silk handkerchief. A lieutenant from the fort had folded his hand and watched the remaining players as he nursed a tumbler of whiskey. The house dealer, a tall, bony man named Christlieb, ignored his cards and chewed on an unlit cigar, and two other men Pete didn't recognize waited for Philley to bet or fold. The two strangers bookended the final player, who Pete couldn't see because of the crowd.

"Let's grab a table and talk business, pard," Pecos said, shoving the greenbacks and silver Robert had given him into his vest pocket. The tall gunman picked up his beer and walked past the poker table toward the wall, followed by Everhart. As Belissari neared the card players, he realized why they had attracted so much attention. The final player was a stunning woman with curly auburn hair and dazzling green eyes.

She wore a brocaded silk dress of blue and silver, low cut in the front with a high neck and black velvet vest. The dress had heavy folds in the front and was gathered at the sides, beaded, and trimmed with lace. She pushed her chair away from the table, and Pete saw a small black purse on her lap. Something glinted inside. A derringer? Probably. Beneath her chair was a satin parasol with a silk lace cover. He also saw that she had managed to kick off her Dieppe tie shoes and was rubbing the arch of her left foot with her right. She wore hose. Pete almost blushed.

"I see that fifty!" Philley shouted. "And raise you twenty!"

Christlieb silently saw the bet. The next player folded and looked at the woman.

She sighed and picked up a blue chip. Noticing Belissari for the first time, she flipped him the chip. "Mister," she said, "would you kiss my chip for luck? I'm having a bad run."

Pete caught the chip in his left hand and felt his face flush. He saw Pecos and Everhart at their table. Buddy was frowning. Everhart's expression said he would have gladly traded places with Pete, but he heard him tell Pecos, "Women can't play poker." Slowly Pete pressed the wooden chip against his lips and tossed it back at the woman, who caught it, smiling, and threw it in the pot.

"There's fifty," she said. She picked up two red chips and slid them into the pot. "There's your twenty.'' And as her smile vanished she added two more blue chips. ''And raise a hundred.''

Pete knew Pecos would be fuming impatiently now, but he wanted to see how this hand played out, and he found himself captivated by the woman gambler. He was glad Hannah wasn't here. She would pretend to be jealous and make him rue the day. He decided he wouldn't tell Hannah about the woman, and he hoped that Pecos and Everhart would keep their mouths shut.

A few spectators gasped at the woman's raise. The other player swore softly and folded, saying, ''It's up to you gents.''

A river of sweat poured down Philley's face. He swallowed a belt of rye, barked out an order for another shot, and wiped his face with his now soggy hanky. Pete had never seen a man sweat so much, and this was January, the false spring of Christmas had been replaced by the more typical winter weather, and although Lightner's was heated, he wouldn't actually call this place warm. He wondered how Philley could handle Presidio in July.

The mercantile owner downed his fresh shot and thumbed through his cards again and again, occasionally staring at the green eyes across the table. ''Them cards ain't gonna change, Ossian,'' a spectator said. ''Bet or fold.''

''Shut up!''

Someone laughed.

Pete turned his attention toward the woman again, then spotted the man standing behind her. He was studying Belissari, frowning. No, it was more than a frown. It was a snarl, like a rabid dog. The man's thumbs hooked his gun belt, which holstered a nickel-plated, double-action Colt on his right hip. He had close-cropped dark hair, a small face, and almost no chin, and wore a black porkpie hat, brown boots, white shirt, and badly tied cravat. His Levi's, held up with dirty canvas suspenders, were about three sizes too large.

Pete Belissari was prejudiced against men in jeans. Those were to be worn by farmers and miners, and Pete was a horseman. No self-respecting *caballero* would ever wear Levi's. Ignoring the poorly clothed, chinless tramp, Pete took another sip of beer and looked at Philley.

"I call," the merchant finally said and threw in a hundred dollars' worth of poker chips.

Christlieb glanced at the woman, smiling, and casually tossed his poker hand into the deadwood, the term for the pile of discarded cards. "You're called, ma'am," the gambler said.

"Full house," she said, placing her five cards on the green felt table. "Queens over fours."

Across the table came a sick groan. Ossian Philley threw down his hand and reached for Christlieb's rye since his own shot glass was empty. Pete stared at the mercantile owner's hand, also a full house, but his was three jacks and two kings—a great poker hand, but it didn't beat three queens and two fours.

Shaking his head in awe, Belissari walked to the table and sat between Everhart and Pecos.

"Got a business proposition for you, pard," Pecos said and drained his mug.

"Dean Everhart here and me are openin' a stage line, run it from Fort Stockton to Fort Davis, to the railroad at Marfa, then down south to Shafter and Presidio.''

Pete nodded. The idea wasn't new to him. When he had met Hannah Scott back in May, she had been neck deep in trouble, fighting a rancher named Rafe Malady who wanted her ranch to run a swing station on his planned stagecoach route from Marfa to Fort Stockton. Rafe Malady was now in prison, and the stage line had fallen through. Apparently, Buddy and Everhart planned to pick up the pieces. What they wanted from Pete, he guessed, was to use Hannah's ranch.

''The ranch is Hannah's, Buddy,'' Pete said. ''She probably wouldn't mind running a swing station. It would bring in some extra money, but you'll have to ask her about that.''

''We intend to, Mr. Belissari,'' Everhart said. ''And I've got lines on swing and home stations already. We'll pick up customers near the ferry at Presidio. The silver mines in Shafter are booming, and we might get a contract to haul payrolls, plus a lot of people are heading there these days. The railroad at Marfa is a natural for business, and the military posts here and at Fort Stockton should also give us plenty of passengers. So you see, I—and my new partner here—have a lot of this already figured out. We should easily get a mail contract too.''

''Where do I come in?'' Pete asked.

''Horses,'' Pecos replied. ''What else?''

Belissari leaned back in his chair and pushed up his hat. Everhart was saying something about owning two stagecoaches, the one out front and another in Presidio, and two teams of mules but, naturally, a lot more stock was needed to run this business. Pete hadn't been into the mountains hunting horses since last spring.

"The post commanders at Forts Davis and Stockton have nothing but high praise for your judge of horseflesh, Mr. Belissari," Everhart said, "as does Buddy and others I have talked to. Buddy and I will be busy trying to set up the business particulars. What we need from you"—he cleared his throat—"are horses."

Pecos grunted something and began rolling a cigarette. "Tell him everything, Dean."

Everhart frowned. "Well, we're also a bit short of capital. What Buddy has proposed is that we go partners. Split everything three ways. We provide the wagons, legal work, stations. You get the horses. I'm told you're a great mustanger."

"You don't want mustangs," Pete said. "Not to pull Concord coaches. You'll need big Americans, and in this country that can be costly. What would you gents think about bringing Hannah into the fold as a partner? That way we'd have more money to work with."

Pete remembered what he had learned about business back at the University of Louisville. Pecos and Everhart were right. A stagecoach line from Presidio to Fort Stockton had a good chance at turning a fast profit. Being part-owner of the line, even for only 25 percent, would provide a lot more clothes and books for those children than whatever Hannah would take in by operating a swing station.

"Miss Scott?" Everhart was incredulous. "A woman can't run a stage line."

Pete knew the comment was coming, and he was well prepared. "A woman can't play poker either."

Pecos cupped his hands and lit his cigarette. Pete could see his friend's lips curl into a smile. Everhart tried to backtrack but failed. He turned to Pecos for help. The gunman lowered his hands, his smile gone, and blew a smoke ring into the air.

"Pretty soon we'll be lettin' 'em vote," Pecos said. He shrugged. "Pete's right. If she wants in, I ain't objectin'."

Slowly, reluctantly, Dean Everhart nodded. Pete was about to get up and order three more beers, though it was still morning and early to be drinking, when Robert the bartender stopped at the table and placed three tumblers of sour mash, his best stock, on the table.

"What have we here?" Everhart asked.

Robert jerked his thumb toward the poker table. The game had broken up. Christlieb was escorting Philley out the front door, the crowd had dispersed, and the man in Levi's was raking the woman's winnings into his ugly hat. Apparently, her luck had turned. While putting on her shoes, she glanced at Pete and smiled. Her green eyes glittered.

"Compliments," he heard Robert answer, "of Miss Jill Coffey."

Chapter Three

Julian Cale owned the ranch bordering Hannah Scott's spread, only his was about four times larger. And while Hannah lived in a small stone and log cabin with five young children, Cale, a bachelor, had a massive Spanish-style house of whitewashed stone surrounded by a high adobe wall. His smokehouse was probably bigger than Hannah's home.

She hooked her left foot on the bottom rail of the corral at Cale's hacienda and stared at the tall horses that pranced for her, their breath white in the cold morning. A bay mare curiously approached her, and she rewarded her with a sugar cube, then patted her forehead. Another, jealous, pawed the earth, moved beside the bay, and demanded a treat, and Hannah pulled out another piece and let the black's coarse tongue take the sugar from her hand. Twelve horses were in this corral, and not a one was smaller than sixteen hands. Every one was a solid color, blacks, bays, and browns, with short legs and well-formed chests, necks, and hindquarters.

"They're Oldenburgs," Julian Cale said behind her, and Hannah turned. Julian Cale was a heavyset man with a sunburned face, thin lips, and cold eyes. He dressed like one of his hired hands, with ducking trousers tucked into stovepipe boots, collarless shirt, woolen vest and high-crowned gray hat. His left arm hung useless at his side, the result of a gunshot wound last summer, but his right hand gripped Hannah's firmly.

Pointing his chin at the horses, Cale said, "They're from Germany originally. Smart horses, but I prefer a good Texas-bred quarter horse for my purposes."

Hannah smiled. "Then you wouldn't mind selling them to me at a dirt-cheap price."

The rancher sent a mouthful of tobacco juice into the dirt and wiped his mouth with the back of his good hand. Hannah liked that. A lot of men would be embarrassed to spit in front of a woman, but not Cale or Buddy Pecos. They treated women fairly—even if Buddy didn't think they should vote. She also enjoyed Cale's deep laugh.

"I heard you were going into the stagecoach business," Cale said. "Figured you'd send Pete to do your horse trading."

"Pete rode out at first light for Presidio. He'll buy some horses, then drop them off at the stations between there and Fort Davis before heading to Fort Stockton to get more stock. I told him I'd see you about horses for our place, and, besides, I'd like to hire one of your cowboys temporarily."

"I see. What do you need a cowhand for?"

"I need help making a bigger corral. We also need to build some sort of bunkhouse to feed the passengers and board any help we hire. My cabin is too small."

Cale laughed again. "Ma'am, you're not going to get any cowboy to do carpentry work or dig fence posts."

"Irwin would."

Irwin Sawyer—his real name was Irwin Stedloe—was a former outlaw who had ridden with the notorious Solomon Wooten. Hannah had known Irwin when they were children back in the Travis County orphanage in Austin, and he had saved her life from Wooten's men, even though he was responsible for her being kidnapped, not to mention Cale's gunshot wound. Irwin also had a huge crush on Hannah—bigger than a crush, actually—but she trusted him, though she hadn't told Pete of her plan.

"You sure, Miss Scott?"

She nodded. "It's up to Irwin. I won't need him long. A month at the most."

"I'll ask him. Now how many horses do you want to buy?"

"How many you willing to part with?"

"Six."

"I need ten."

"Six Oldenburgs, and I'll find four good harness horses." He shook his head. "I have to admit, Miss Scott, that I'm not much of a stagecoach man. Riding in those bone-busters makes me sick."

"Pete's the same way. But Buddy Pecos lets him ride on top, and he doesn't get sick up there. Maybe you should try it."

"No thanks. Like I said, I prefer my Texas quarter horses." He spit again, looked intently at the animals while working his tobacco, and said, "Two hundred twenty for each Oldenburg, and four hundred total for the others. Your pick of each. That's"—he looked skyward as his mouth moved silently—"make it seventeen hundred even. You paying cash, gold, or bank draft?"

Hannah laughed. "Mr. Cale, are you trying to take advantage of an unmarried woman with five orphans? I think we should haggle some."

Cale shook his head. "Those Oldenburgs come all the way from northwest Germany. They're hard to come by in these parts. Two twenty is, like you said, 'dirt cheap.' "

She didn't say anything for a minute, opened her mouth but paused, and looked back at the corral, letting him think she was actually considering his offer. Finally, she faced him and said, "Word is you won them in a faro game."

A grunt followed another stream of tobacco juice. His eyes locked on Hannah's, and his lips formed a smile.

"All right, Miss Scott, let's start haggling."

Pete Belissari left Poseidon at Van Boskirk's stables near the courthouse and walked toward the restaurant bordering Lempert's Addition. His stomach told him that the coffee he drank at dawn before leaving the ranch wouldn't sustain him on the trail, and the chef at Lempert's had a way with biscuits, thick, hot buttermilk wonders with chopped pecans mixed in. Belissari's morning had been busy—he had a letter of reference from Captain Jack Leslie at Fort Davis, a bank draft, and now Poseidon was getting a new shoe on his left forefoot—so he deserved a good breakfast before riding out for Presidio and meeting Cash Hardee. He was walking to an empty table when a voice stopped him.

"Join me?"

Jill Coffey sat alone at a table by a window, delicately holding a porcelain coffee cup. Placing the cup on its matching saucer, she stood and held out her right hand. She wore a French-style walking costume, with white flannel skirt and royal blue polonaise, trimmed with red velvet ribbon bows and nickel-plated buckles. The blue jacket was double-breasted with buttons the size of eggs, and her hat was of fine Milan straw with a beaded edge and faced with a red ribbon and flowers. Her gorgeous eyes were hypnotic, and Pete took her hand and smiled. He briefly thought of Hannah but decided there was no harm in eating breakfast with Jill Coffey.

"I didn't thank you for the sour mash," he said, and helped Jill into her chair. He saw the small purse in the chair beside her, and this time got a good look at the silver-plated Remington derringer. Pete sat facing her and ordered coffee, biscuits, and ham, then realized he hadn't introduced himself.

"My name's Pete Belissari."

"Pleased to know you, Pete Belissari. I'm Jill Coffey."

He bowed slightly, paused as the Mexican waiter poured his coffee and refilled Jill's mug, then smiled stupidly because he couldn't think of a thing to say.

"Belissari? Italian?"

"Greek."

"You have no accent."

"Lost it in college. The University of Louisville in Kentucky."

"I see. You're a long way from the sea, Pete. I thought all Greeks became fishermen or sailors."

"I'm a horseman," he said. "My father is the seaman."

"A horseman? As in stealing them?" She smiled.

"Catching and breaking mustangs, actually," he said, returning the grin.

He was amazed at how easy the conversation was going. Sipping her coffee, she studied him with those eyes, and finally commented, "So you're college educated, the son of a Greek seaman, and you make your living in this wasteland in the middle of nowhere. Strange, I think, that a man like you would sell yourself so short."

She was blunt. Pete liked that. "It seemed Homeric at the time," he replied, and she laughed.

"I thought gamblers slept in," he said after the waiter had brought their food and left.

"The early bird . . ." she said, but didn't finish the cliché. She picked up her fork, and Pete followed her lead. They ate in silence, and when they were finished, the waiter refilled their coffee cups.

"I have a poker game to attend at Lightner's Saloon this morning," she said. "We have an opening if you'd care to join us."

He shook his head. "I'm leaving for Presidio today, and I'm not much for saloon poker."

"You don't gamble?"

"Working with horses is enough of a gamble for me," he said. "Oh, I'll play a hand of poker with friends, but in a public place with strangers? That can get ugly."

"That's why I have Tubac."

Pete remembered the chinless gunman from the other day. He thought that a woman with Jill Coffey's wardrobe could do a lot better than having Tubac for a bodyguard but he kept his mouth shut.

"It's just as well, Pete," she said. "I play to win. If you played cards against me, we might not be friends. That's why they call me—"

"The Black Widow."

She laughed. "You've heard of me. Strange, I didn't think you were the five-penny Western type."

"I prefer the classics," he said, "but there's this seven-year-old who is helping keep the Wide Awake Library in business."

"Your son?"

"No ma'am."

"You're not married?"

He shook his head.

"So perhaps you'll be able to dine with me when you return from Presidio."

The coffee turned a tad bitter. Had he been flirting? He was like his father in that respect. He couldn't help himself. Yes, Jill Coffey was a beautiful woman, but . . .

"I . . ." he hesitated.

Jill shook her head. "I see," she said. "There's some schoolmarm you're wooing."

He gave a half-shrug, half-nod. "Something like that."

"That's too bad, Pete," she said. "I think the two of us could have had an enjoyable evening, but I'm not really a 'Black Widow.' You wouldn't mind escorting me to Lightner's now, would you, dear? I think Tubac is sleeping off a quart of whiskey."

He insisted on paying for breakfast—after all, Jill had treated him to Kentucky sour mash—and, with her arm hooked in his, led her through the doors at Lightner's. Slick Slaughter was at the bar, and Pete saw

Ossian Philley, already sweating, at the table along with Langford Christlieb. A faro dealer from Marfa played solitaire to kill time, and two Fort Davis businessmen sipped their morning rye and counted their chips.

"Thanks for breakfast, Pete," Jill said. "Good luck in Presidio."

"Good luck to you," he said. They shook hands, and she walked to her place at the table. Pete turned to leave when Dean Everhart swung through the doors and almost knocked him down.

"I thought you were in Fort Stockton," Belissari said angrily after regaining his balance.

"And you're supposed to be in Presidio."

"I'm riding out now. And you?"

Everhart looked past him toward the poker table. Belissari frowned. "I thought I'd try my luck against the Black Widow," he said. "*Women can't play poker,* remember?"

Belissari sighed and walked to the livery. "Partners can take the fun out of business," he said to himself. But he couldn't worry too much about Dean Everhart. He pulled the letter from his coat pocket, studied it, and remembered what the Army doctor had told him earlier that morning.

"You ever dealt with Cash Hardee, son?" Jack Leslie asked as he wrote the letter in his office at the post hospital.

"Not personally."

"He's a hard man. The Mexicans in Presidio call him *Un Mal Hombre.* If you do manage to buy some horses from him, check the brands. He probably stole most of his stock from the other side of the Rio Grande.''

Pete smiled. It was an old game, often deadly, along the border. Texans raided south for horses and cattle. Mexicans returned the favor, although the Texas Rangers and *Rurales* and *Federales* were cutting down on that traffic. In the old days, rumor had it that Cash Hardee bought stolen horses from Comanches and Apaches. Some even said he traded whiskey and firearms with the Indians. Still, if a man in West Texas needed enough horses to operate a stage line, Cash Hardee was the only man to see.

When the ink was dry, Leslie folded the letter and handed it to Pete, who carefully put it inside his coat. He thanked the doctor, who only shrugged.

''I'm not sure it'll do you any good, Pete. The Army has bought horses from Hardee before, but that was during the height of the Apache wars when we both needed each other. These days, he needs no one—unless he's in a killing mood.''

Chapter Four

Hannah sat on a stool next to the bed and placed the back of her hand against Paco's forehead. The seven-year-old fireball was feverish, and he opened his dark, puppy-dog eyes and frowned. Like most boys, he loathed being sick, especially with so much excitement going on. Outside, Irwin Sawyer, Chris, and even little Bruce were busy building a larger corral, lean-to, and covered patio to feed passengers or hired help once the first stage came through. They had opted against building a bunkhouse to save money.

"Oh, precious," Hannah said. "How are you feeling?"

He shrugged and sighed.

"Would you like me to read to you?"

Now his eyes lighted up and he nodded excitedly. "You gonna read from one of Pete's Greek books, Mama Hannah? Pete was reading to me before he left about this Trojan horse. Them Greeks hid in this wooden horse and then came out and surprised the Trojans and started hacking 'em to pieces. It was real good."

Hannah laughed. "Honey," she said, "I can't read Pete's Greek books. But I have this." She held up the large hardbound book she had ordered from the latest *Montgomery Ward & Co. Catalogue and Buyers' Guide.*

"What's that?"

"Charles Dickens. Remember? We read his novel about Scrooge and the ghosts on Christmas Eve."

"Yeah, that was pretty good."

"This is good too." She opened the book and began, skipping the preface: "Chapter One. The Period. It was the best of times, it was the worst of times, it was the age of wisdom, it was—"

Paco's frown cut her short. She slowly closed *A Tale of Two Cities* and put the book on the bed. "You don't want to hear this? Even Pete likes Charles Dickens."

"Oh, it's fine, Mama Hannah, but I wonder if you could read me something else."

"Such as?"

He reached under his pillow and pulled out a handful of thin, poorly bound pulp novels. Hannah took them, scanning the titles—*Fancy Frank of Colorado; or, The Trapper's Trust . . . The Crimson Trail; or, On Custer's Last Warpath* "as witnessed by W. F. Cody" . . . *Wild Times in Wichita; or, An Ace for the Black Widow.*

"Most boys your age when they get a nickel, they buy a piece of candy. You like your half-dime novels, don't you?"

"Some of 'em cost a whole dime now, Mama Hannah."

"Well, I'll read some from one of these—but only because you're sick," and she tossed two paperbacks on top of *A Tale of Two Cities* and glanced at the cover of *Wild Times in Wichita,* published by The Five Cent Wide Awake Library and written by Colonel L. Merryweather Handal. The woodcut engraving on the cover showed a woman in a black dress and wide-brimmed sombrero firing a revolver across a card table. Sighing, Hannah opened the book and read:

Chapter One
The Black Widow Bucks The Tiger

Jill Coffey's heart pounded like cannonfire as she studied the faro layout at Texas Jack's Gambling Palace. Wild Bill Hickok, the prince of pistoleers, dealt for the house. Trying their luck against him were Billy the Kid, Buffalo Bill Cody, Kit Carson and a man wearing a fake beard whom she, and only she, recognized from their brief romance in Kansas City.

Jesse James!

She steeled her nerves until her blood turned colder than ice and her green eyes hardened like lead. If she could beat these gents at their own game, faro, she, Jill Coffey, would be the queen of the West—and she'd teach Jesse James, that famous outlaw, a lesson in manners.

"Gentlemen," she said, and skillfully found her chips. "May I join you? . . ."

Hannah stopped as the door to the cabin opened. Paco had already fallen asleep. She checked his forehead again and pulled the blanket up over his shoulders. Chris was tiptoeing toward her.

"Mama Hannah," he whispered, "you had better come outside."

* * *

The Chinati Mountains had been a barren, desolate piece of real estate when Pete Belissari first saw the Big Bend country, and he never expected anyone would settle in this desert between Presidio and Marfa. In less than a year, however, a town had sprung up near Cibolo Creek. The hand-painted sign read: WELCOME TO SHAFTER.

Adobe and stone houses, from wretched hovels to near mansions, lined Main Street, which was fed by a couple of smaller streets and several dusty alleys. A Catholic church had already opened, and a Protestant one was under construction. There were stores, a small jail, a line of saloons, and a long adobe bunkhouse called The Men's Clubhouse, where single miners lived, compliments of the Presidio Mining Company and its new ore reduction mill.

An Army teamster named Spencer had discovered silver deposits back in 1880, and talked three other men, including William R. Shafter, into going into business with him. Shafter had been the commanding officer at Fort Davis, a fat, arrogant, foul-mouthed colonel of the First Infantry. Pete loathed Colonel Shafter and was much happier when Benjamin Grierson became the commanding officer late in '82.

Grierson was a cavalryman, a pleasant gentleman who let his staff officers do what they thought best, within reason. As a mustanger, Belissari had profited under Grierson's command, selling mustangs to the Tenth Cavalry until the Army finally ceased buying his horses last year.

Now William Shafter was growing rich from the Shafter Mine, even had a town named after him. In '82, Shafter, Spencer, and the other two partners joined forces with Daniel Cook, a California businessman whose specialty was mining. The Presidio Mining Company was incorporated, and last spring the silver mines became a big business.

With luck, Belissari, Hannah, Buddy, and Everhart would also profit here.

He drifted down Main Street, crossed Cibolo Creek, and followed the road south, reining in Poseidon at a hardscrabble outfit on the edge of town. A big corral, lean-to, and barn stood behind a crumbling adobe house. Leaning against the wall under the freshly painted sign that read SHAFTER STATION was Buddy Pecos.

"You took your sweet time gettin' here," Pecos said, and drenched a scorpion with tobacco juice.

The two friends shook hands, and Pete unsaddled Poseidon and let him cool off before leading him to the water trough. Belissari washed his face and examined the old house that would serve as the first swing station on the way from Presidio. Pecos pried the plug of tobacco from his cheek and put it in his hat to save for later. Then he turned toward the house and yelled, "Hey, Goldy, get your lazy carcass out here—and bring McBride!"

A tall, thin, clean-shaven man in canvas trousers and a homespun shirt stepped into the sun. A shorter man with long gray hair grasped the tall man's right arm and was led toward the water trough. Pete frowned. It was obvious that the gray-headed man was blind.

Pecos introduced Pete to David Goldman and Happy Jack McBride, owners of Shafter Station. Goldman was new to West Texas. Born in Missouri, he had worked on Ben Holladay's Overland Stage Line on the Salt Lake City–Folsom route during the '60s, so he had more than just passing knowledge of what was expected of him as the manager of a swing station.

Happy Jack, Belissari was informed, had been in Texas all his life. He had worked for John Butterfield's stage company as a driver, served with Sibley in the War, and, like Pete, had hunted wild mustangs in the mountains before a band of Apaches blinded him with hot coals and left him for dead near Rattlesnake Springs.

"But, pard, he's still the best judge of horses I know of," Pecos said, "and I know you."

Pete nodded politely. Goldy laughed. "I think he needs convincing, Buddy."

"Yep."

Happy Jack also smiled. "Make it worth my while."

"Bet a silver dollar, Pete," Pecos said, "that Happy Jack can tell what color Poseidon is."

"You've told him already."

"Nope. My word. But you can pick any other horse if you want. From the corral, or bring one in from town."

Pete decided to play along. He pulled out a coin and handed it to Pecos. "Show me," he said.

David Goldman led McBride to Poseidon, and the blind man patted the horse's neck and slowly began rubbing the mane, flank and back of the mustang. Pete tugged on his mustache, patiently waiting on the game—or joke—to end so he could go inside, warm himself by the fireplace, and maybe have a drink before supper.

A man could die of thirst out here, he thought. But he said nothing.

Finally, Happy Jack stepped back and said, "You have a fine horse here, Mr. Belissari. Good stock. Smart too. He can carry a man far, won't quit on you, and got just the right amount of temperament to keep you on your toes. Reminds me of a mustang I caught in the Sierra Madres back in '68 or '69. Sold him to the great Cochise, and that's the gospel truth."

"What color is he?" Pete asked.

"Aw, shucks, sonny. That's easy. He's a gray. Where's my dollar?"

Dean Everhart was leaning against the limestone well in the front yard, slaking his thirst. He saw Hannah, tossed the ladle into the oak bucket, and slowly walked toward her. Two strangers were busy hitching the team of mules to Everhart's stagecoach, while another man ordered them from horseback. Irwin Sawyer ignored them and continued to dig post holes while Bruce and the two orphan girls watched.

Hannah told Chris to go help Irwin. The man on the horse turned toward her, smiled, and tipped his ugly hat. He was an ugly man—he didn't even have a chin—and those two with him weren't much better. One was a black man with a massive beard still in his Army duds though he had been drummed out of the service at Fort Davis more than six months ago. The other was a ne'er-do-well who hung around the saloons in town.

"Mr. Everhart." Hannah's tone was noncommittal. "What's going on?"

"Oh, a bit of a setback, Miss Scott."

"What are these men doing with your coach?"

He took a deep breath. "Well, ma'am, it's their stagecoach now. I, uh, well, I was playing some poker with Jill Coffey and had a pretty good hand, but, uh, well, they call her the Black Widow and, uh, ma'am, I had two pair . . . well, you don't know poker, but, uh—"

"Excuse me, Mr. Everhart. Did you say *Jill Coffey*?"

"Yes, ma'am. She's got quite a reputation."

"Go on."

"Anyway, I lost the Concord—this one, not the one I have down in Presidio—to the Black Widow. That's what them dime novels call her. Lost the mules too, but that ain't much of a loss.

"I swear—pardon, ma'am—but I was sure my hand was a winner. Two pair, kings up, I knew I had her dead, but she has a way with them pastecards. By jingo, I think she's cheatin' me, but I sure couldn't prove it."

"You gonna withdraw that remark, mister."

The words chilled Hannah as Dean Everhart stumbled, turned around, and faced the sorry-looking gunman who stood close enough that Hannah could smell the whiskey on his breath and stink on his clothes. The team was hitched to the Concord, and the two ruffians were ready to go, their mounts tied up short behind the stagecoach. This man, with his right hand resting on the butt of his revolver, was ready for something else.

"Tubac, I didn't mean nothin'," Everhart pleaded.

"You take back what you said about Miss Jill, you old skinflint, or I'm gonna shoot you dead in front of this swell-lookin' gal and them kids."

"Tubac, I ain't wearin' a gun!"

"Makes no nevermind to me."

"I didn't mean nothin', Tubac. I apologize."

"I don't think you mean it."

"I mean it, Tubac. I swear I mean it. I apologize."

The gunman smiled. "Get on your hands and beg. Convince me."

Hannah stepped off the porch between the two men. Her eyes flamed.

"He apologized. Now you and those men are getting off my property. You're not going to shoot anybody, you're not going to threaten anybody, and nobody is going to get on his knees for the likes of you. Get moving!"

Tubac's smile widened. "Feisty," he said. "I likes that."

The smile vanished though when Irwin Sawyer said, "Is there a problem, Hannah?"

Tubac turned suddenly but froze. Irwin held his post-hole diggers like an ax, and his firm expression let the gunman know he could crush his skull before he'd ever get that Colt out of the holster.

Hannah caught her breath. "These men were just leaving, Irwin. Thank you."

Tubac's right hand strayed from his revolver, and he faced Hannah again, smiling. "Be seein' you, ma'am," he said, tipping his hat as he walked to his horse. Irwin handed the hardware to Everhart and pulled a Colt revolver from his waistband, just in case

Tubac tried something, but the gunman only yelled at the men in the stagecoach.

The Concord took off, and Tubac mounted his buckskin mare and followed with an oath and a final, cold glare.

Chapter Five

It is said that Cash Hardee used human blood instead of water to make adobe, which would explain the reddish tint of the walls at Fort Leaton. Pete Belissari knew it was only a myth, but still he couldn't shake the feeling that haunted him as he walked Poseidon toward the giant fortress a few miles southeast of Presidio.

Actually, Fort Leaton had been built long before Cash Hardee discovered it. The Mexicans said Spanish soldiers constructed the fort in the late 1700s before abandoning it in the early part of the nineteenth century. It had lain in ruins for more than thirty years when Ben Leaton bought the property in 1848 and used it as his home and trading post until his death in '51.

Now Cash Hardee lived there, as he had for ten years, ruling his land near the Rio Grande like some feudal despot. Even the Texas Rangers left him alone.

Four massive adobe walls enclosed the entire complex, with heavy wooden doors and shutters, each window crisscrossed with well-secured cane strips that prevented anyone from entering . . . or leaving. Fort Leaton had been, and still was, impregnable.

Pete pounded on the main door that overlooked the floodplain below. Two well-armed guards eyed him curiously from their posts on the roof before the door creaked open and a Mexican boy, about Chris's age, stepped forward, took Poseidon's reins, and led him to the corral in the back. Belissari walked through the *placita* and leaned against a massive ox cart, watched the boy with his horse, and waited.

Goats and chickens wandered freely, an elderly woman milked a thin, leathery cow, and two vaqueros laughed and rolled cigarettes as they sat on the top rail of a fence. Inside the corral were two dozen horses. Big Americans. Near the blacksmith's shop was an old stagecoach that, incredibly, looked to be in as poor condition as Everhart's, maybe even worse. Pete looked up at the roof. The two guards kept their focus on him, their rifles ready.

"Buenos tardes, señor. ¿En qué puedo servirle?"

A dark, ancient man with stark white hair and long goatee stood patiently in cotton clothes and wooden sandals. Belissari ran the Spanish through his head and answered, *"¿Esta el señor Hardee?"*

"¿Por qué?"

"Me gustaría comprar caballos."

"¡Bueno!" the man said, smiling. "We have many fine horses to sell. I will tell *El Patrón* that you are here. May I have your name?"

Pete answered, handing over his letter of introduction, and the man disappeared inside one of the compound's many rooms. In a few minutes, he reappeared at the doorway and motioned him to follow. Pete was glad to get inside. The old Mexican's sandals clopped against the hard floor, echoing off dark walls that lined the wide hallway. They passed through several spartan rooms until his guide opened another thick door and motioned for Pete to step inside. Belissari felt like Edmond Dantes being led to his dungeon at Château d'If in Alexandre Dumas's *The Count of Monte Cristo*, one of Pete's favorite novels.

Pete stepped inside. "*Uno momento, señor* Belissari," the man said. "*Espere aquí.*" The door closed behind him. The shutter was open, allowing light and a cold breeze to fill the room. Wood crackled in a fireplace in the corner. In the center of the room he saw a roundtop, black-enameled iron trunk in front of a high, rolltop desk of solid oak. Two chairs sat in front of the desk with another, larger and made of leather, behind it. An oak lounge covered with a plush rug was positioned near the fireplace, and a cabinet stood against the far wall. The room had more furniture than the rest of the fort combined.

Then he saw the lance hanging horizontally above the fireplace. The weapon was long and thin, red-brown wood painted black near the tip with red streamers of cotton fastened just below the dark, iron point. Small feathers were tied to each end of cloth. It was an Apache war lance, but what drew Pete's attention were the three strips of human hair, cured and black, tied to the spear with sinew, hanging over the mantel like a trophy deer's antlers.

"The Sonoran government would have paid me two hundred and fifty pesos for them some years back," a voice drawled. "But I liked those too much to sell."

Pete hadn't even heard the man open the door. Cash Hardee walked to the cabinet, opened it, pulled out a bottle, and filled two crystal whiskey tumblers. He strode across the room to Pete and handed him a glass, then pointed to the scalps with his drink.

"The one on the left belonged to one of Cochise's top lieutenants. I killed him with my bare hands in the Dragoon Mountains in '63." He pointed to a rugged scar that crossed his forehead. "Earned this lovely trophy. The middle one I took off a warrior I shot with a Rolling Block rifle at eight hundred yards in the Sierra Madres ten years ago. And the other belonged to this Mimbres I took for a wife for a few months in '71 or '72." He downed his whiskey, looked Pete in the eye and said coldly, "She tried to double-cross me."

Cash Hardee was a tall, tan man, square shouldered and solid, with short brown hair and a thick mustache peppered with gray. He would have been handsome if not for his wild, frightening eyes, a blue so pale they seemed transparent.

He wore *calzoneras,* the open-sided pants favored by vaqueros, of black broadcloth with brass buttons and scalloped leather seat and thighs, Apache-style moccasins the same as Pete's, a bib front shirt of navy flannel and ivory buttons, cream silk bandanna, and red sash. Tucked inside the sash were a scalping knife and brace of open-top Colts, nickel plated with Tiffany grips.

Hardee held up his empty glass. "Your reputation precedes you, Pete Belissari. *"¡A su salud!"*

Belissari responded to the Spanish toast in Greek. *"Yiá chará,"* he said, then translated: "Health and joy." He swallowed a couple of fingers of the amber liquid, suppressed a cough and gag as the whiskey—if one could call it whiskey—burned a fiery path to his stomach.

Cash Hardee refilled his own glass and sat behind

his desk, gesturing at one of the smaller chairs for Pete. Once both men were seated, Hardee's eyes locked on the mustanger. "So you want to buy horses? How many?"

"Plenty," Pete said and began explaining what he needed for the stage line. Hardee never blinked, his expression never changed, and he never sipped his cocktail while Pete talked. Belissari had traded horses with Army officers, Texas Rangers, stubborn skinflint ranchers, Indians, and outlaws—but no one made him feel as uncomfortable as Cash Hardee. He finished talking, sipped his rotgut, and waited.

A piece of wood popped like a gunshot in the fireplace, startling Pete so much that he almost spilled his drink. But it didn't bother Hardee. The wind began to moan outside, thunder rolled in the distance, a hawk gave a shrill cry. Finally his host drained the whiskey as if it were water on a hot day, tugged on his mustache, and said, "You have a nice head of hair, Pete Belissari."

Pete recovered after a second and nodded uncertainly, thinking of Hannah and her fruitless attempts to get him to reduce the mane that hung past his shoulders. He told her that old-timers wore their hair long to taunt scalp-hunting Indians. Hannah scoffed. He told her that it kept him warm in the winter and the sun off his neck in the summer. She called him Samson. He replied, honestly, that he just didn't like, or trust, barbers.

Hardee quoted: " 'But the very hairs of your head are all numbered.' Matthew 10.30."

Pete's face was blank. Hardee smiled and commented, "Darken it a bit, grease it some, and your scalp could pass for an Apache's."

Slowly Pete crossed his leg for no reason other than to feel the reassuring weight of the Colt revolver holstered on his right hip. He had no idea what Hardee was talking about, if the man was joking, toying with him, interested in adding to his collection of human hair, or just completely mad.

Hardee found an elegant, gold-plated case in one of the cubicles in his desk, opened it, and pulled out two long cigars. After tossing Pete one, he bit off the end of another, jammed it in his mouth, struck a match with his thumbnail, and after a few seconds blew a thin trail of blue smoke toward the ceiling.

"I think we can do business, Pete Belissari. You'll sup with me tonight. I insist. And afterward, we'll play poker."

"You may be a good horseman, Pete Belissari—second to me, perhaps, because I'm the best judge of horseflesh, bronc rider, and caballero in these parts—but you ain't much with the pastecards." Hardee smiled, knocked a long cigar ash onto the floor, and threw a heavy leather pouch onto the center of the table.

"I see your nickel," he added, "and raise you fifteen hundred dollars in gold."

Sighing heavily, Pete leaned back. They had dined on *cordero asado,* onions, carrots, bread, and red wine with a Mexican pastry for dessert. And during the course of the meal, the two men had talked pleasantly about horses and the stagecoach business. Now they were three hours into a late card game, and Pete knew why he disliked gambling with strangers. The biggest bet either had made previously had been a dollar; now Hardee was trying to buy the pot, which had been less than four dollars.

Buddy Pecos once said that two-handed poker was about as fun as rolling through prickly pear in your longhandles.

Belissari looked at his cards. They were playing five-card stud, dealing the first card down and the next four up, betting after each up card. ''Texas rules,'' Hardee had declared. ''None of that lily gal poker with straights and flushes, that nonsense. Pairs, three, four of a kind, full houses. Good old-fashioned poker.''

The cards were old, their backs trimmed with gold and engraved patriotically with American flags, a red, white, and blue shield and blue anchor. Belissari's up cards were the ten of diamonds, jack of hearts, four of spades, and three of diamonds—hardly worth fifteen hundred dollars. But his hole card was the jack of clubs, giving him a good pair in five-card stud.

Hardee's cards showing were the six of spades, nine of diamonds, seven of spades, and king of spades—also not worth a sizable bet. Belissari had raised since pairing up his jack with the third card. Hardee's last card up was the king, but he hadn't paired up. Pete knew this because he had noticed earlier in the night that the top left corner of the ace of clubs had been filed down and slightly torn. That was Cash Hardee's hole card now.

Pete took a long drag on his cigar. He didn't really consider this cheating. He hadn't marked the card, just merely noticed it as any good poker player would.

Hardee was bluffing or maybe thinking that Belissari had no pairs and his ace-king would win.

Slowly Pete reached into pocket and withdrew his bank draft and tossed it on the table. Hardee eyed it casually and asked, "You raising?"

If it had been anyone else, he would have increased the bet, but Pete didn't want to anger his host too much. Taking him for a small fortune in gold was enough. He shook his head and said, "Call. I'll make change."

Hardee nodded. He scooped up his down card and slapped his meaty right hand on the table, lifted it and revealed—to Pete's horror—a shiny, sickening king of diamonds.

El Patrón of Fort Leaton laughed, rang a bell on the table, and ground out his cigar with the heel of his moccasin on the cold floor. Pete lifted the king of diamonds and studied it. There was no small tear, no worn corner. How could he have made such a mistake?

"Like I said, Pete Belissari," Hardee said. "You ain't one for cards. Now I'm guessing that you don't have any money to even talk about buying horses, so tomorrow morn we'll ride over to the Presidio bank and you can cash that draft and pay me." The white-haired Mexican servant appeared. Hardee issued some instructions in Spanish and told Belissari, "Tadeo will show you to your room. It's been a pleasure."

His head hurt. Only part of that money had been his. *People go to jail for things like this.* Had Hardee been cheating? Setting him up? Pete picked up the deck of cards and followed the servant. Left alone in his room, a cold, damp prison that smelled of goats,

Pete lit a lantern and counted the cards. Fifty-one, and missing was the ace of clubs. So, Cash Hardee was a cheater.

Not that Pete could do anything about it.

Pete pulled Poseidon to a stop near the bank. Hardee rode past him a few yards, then reined up and turned around. "Delaying it won't help, Pete Belissari," Hardee said with a smile.

Belissari returned the smile. He had thought about challenging Hardee, showing him the short deck of cards—though he could prove nothing in a courtroom—but Hardee had brought six riders with him, each armed with revolvers, knives, and rifles, and Pete had devised a better plan.

"I was just wondering if you'd be interested in doubling your earnings, or more?" Pete asked pleasantly.

The man called *Un Mal Hombre* stroked his mustache. "Go on."

"I bet I know a better judge of horseflesh than you." He paused, letting the challenge sink in before continuing. "Just north of here, at Shafter Station, is a blind man who can tell the color of a horse just by touching it."

Hardee responded with an oath and long laugh.

"You bring the horse," Pete said. "If he guesses the color, I get back my bank draft, the fifteen hundred you put up last night and another thousand to make it interesting."

Now the old scalphunter licked his lips. "And what will you put up?"

"When we met, you said my reputation preceded

me. Then I assume you have heard of Duck Pegasus and Lightning Flash."

Hardee's crazy eyes blinked rapidly. Almost everyone in West Texas had heard of those two horses. Pete added, "They're worth a good deal more than four thousand dollars."

Poseidon snorted. Pete waited. Hardee laughed again, and finally shouted, "All right, *señor*, it's a bet! I'll be at Shafter Station tomorrow morning. But if this is some trick, if you think you can double-cross me, my friend, remember my Mimbres wife."

Chapter Six

"You bet what?"

Pete wilted underneath Buddy Pecos's one-eyed stare. He took off his hat, ran his fingers through his hair, and told Pecos everything that had happened at Fort Leaton. The tall gunman was not sympathetic.

"That's the dumbest thing I ever heard. You ain't that stupid."

"What was I supposed to do?"

"If you thought Hardee was cheatin', fold your hand. Don't never bet into somethin' like that."

"I didn't think he was cheating. Anyway, we can get the money back, and more. All Happy Jack has to do is guess the color—and he can do that . . . can't he?"

"Yeah, sure. He tells by the touch. Says each color has a different texture. But that ain't our problem. Our problem is gonna be keepin' Hardee from killin' us once he loses the bet."

Pete dropped into a rough-hewn chair next to a wooden camp table on the makeshift porch of Shafter Station. He hadn't slept well at all, dreading this morning, wondering what would happen if Cash Hardee won his bet. David Goldman sat across from him, going through the mail: a couple of letters, the latest edition of *The Presidio County News*, and a Beadle's Dime Library novel that caught his eye.

Sabine Savage;
or, The Pard of the Black Widow
Being a True Account of the Noted Texas Duelist,
Sergeant Owen "Sabine" Savage,
And His Fights with Mexican Border Gangs
By Colonel Noble Zane

Pete picked up the paperback, snorted at the ridiculous woodcut engraving of the hero, protecting the handsome Jill Coffey, fending off a dozen sombrero-clad bandits with poorly illustrated revolvers and a giant bowie knife. He tossed the book on the table and looked at the headline on the newspaper.

Jill Coffey in Town
Noted Gambler Graces
Our Gaming Establishments.
Her Beauty Is Well-Known,
As Is Her Expertiese
with Cards.
Exclusive Interview!

"Expertise is spelled wrong," Pete said, and read:

Jill Coffey, late of Fort Worth, has set up a gambling table at Lightner's Saloon in our fair town on her way to San Francisco. The heroine, or some say witch, of many five-penny Westerns, has earned the unhappy nickname of the Black

Widow, but this editor found her to be charming, polite and a fine specimen of the fairer sex who has donated a portion of her winnings to various needy causes and is also interested in forming a stagecoach line, which might make things interesting for another party trying to form such a business.

He stopped reading. Stagecoach line? That didn't ease his anxiety. A quick scan of the rest of the article revealed no further mention of Coffey's stage line, and Belissari folded the paper and sighed. Cash Hardee. Jill Coffey. Pete's problems kept multiplying. But he pushed thoughts of Coffey aside and concentrated on Hardee, who would be arriving at any minute. His glance fell on the cover of the dime novel, then lifted and locked on Goldman, who looked up, stuck a letter in his pocket, and frowned.

"What is it?"

Pete tugged on his mustache. He pointed at the novel. "You ever heard of Sabine Savage?"

Goldman laughed. "Belissari, these books ain't real. I just get 'em to read to Happy Jack. He likes the action. There ain't no such person as Sabine Savage or Jill Coffey."

"There is a Jill Coffey," Pete corrected and tapped his finger on the newspaper. "And you're going to become Sabine Savage as long as Cash Hardee is here."

"Huh?"

Pete didn't have much time to explain. "You read these things," he said, pointing at the novel. "You know how these guys are supposed to act. Just sit here, look mean, and don't say a word.''

Quickly he stood, swiped Buddy Pecos's new black Stetson, and planted it low on Goldman's head, though it was a size too big. Next he found two empty whiskey bottles inside, filled them with tea and placed them in front of Goldman, along with a beaten-up .44 Remington that dated to the War and probably hadn't been fired since Lee's surrender.

''This ain't gonna scare Cash Hardee,'' Pecos said.

''No,'' Pete replied, ''but it might make his gunmen a tad uneasy.'' For the next hour, Goldman sipped tea and practiced looking mean, Buddy Pecos cleaned his rifle, and Happy Jack McBride slept peacefully on his cot. Pete pranced around the yard like a nervous stallion. Finally, he spotted dust rising down the road to Presidio. Belissari walked to Goldman, picked up *The Presidio County News* and fanned himself, though it was cold.

''Remember,'' Pete said, ''you're Sabine Slaughter, fearless gunman.''

''Sabine Savage,'' Pecos corrected, slipping a long cartridge into his single-shot rifle.

Belissari swallowed. Cash Hardee was riding into the yard, pulling a horse completely covered in blankets and followed by ten riders who looked to be advertising an arsenal.

Pete offered Hardee a cup of coffee, but *Un Mal Hombre* was in poor humor this morning. Belissari had hoped Hardee would have been in a good mood, expecting to win his bet, but the killer had left Fort Leaton before daybreak and his fuse was short after the long ride. His clothes, from his striped britches and

Mexican-style corduroy jacket to his wide-brimmed tan hat, were caked with dust. His eyes flamed as his raw voice cracked: "Bring out that blind man, Pete Belissari."

Belissari nodded at Pecos, who disappeared inside the shack and reappeared a few seconds later leading Happy Jack McBride toward the blanketed horse.

"Cash Hardee," Pete said pleasantly when Happy and Pecos were beside him, "this is Happy Jack McBride, the best judge of horses you'll ever meet, and Buddy Pecos, the former sheriff of Presidio County." He looked for a reaction, but saw none. "And at the table is Sergeant Owen 'Sabine' Slaughter, the famed Texas duelist and friend of Jill Coffey, the Black Widow."

Hardee snorted, but Pete continued. "Miss Coffey is in Fort Davis, and Sergeant Slaughter just rode down to visit us." He handed the newspaper to Hardee, who scanned it before dismounting. Hardee stood in front of Happy Jack, studying the old-timer, making sure he was indeed blind, while Pete handed the newspaper and dime novel to Pecos.

"I told you it wouldn't work," Pecos whispered.

"Just pass the book and paper around those gunmen of his," Pete said. "Talk him up. Make those guys think twice about getting into a shooting scrape with Buddy Pecos and Sabine Slaughter."

"Savage," Pecos corrected again. "Slaughter's our fine new sheriff."

"You ready to start this fandango?" Hardee said.

"Sure," Pete replied and turned to face his guest. "You bring the money and draft?"

"Yes, I did. But I don't see no Lightning Flash and Duck Pegasus in that corral!"

"They're both at the ranch north of Fort Davis. Didn't have time to ride there and bring them back by today, but if I lose, you can ride with me and I'll give you the horses, bill of sale, and treat you to supper." Pete smiled. Hardee didn't. Pete added, "But I'm not going to lose."

"Tomás!" Hardee barked. "Carlos! Take the blankets off that nag!"

Two vaqueros dismounted and began working on the ropes securing the blankets. Pete looked around. Pecos was talking to a couple of Hardee's riders, while Goldy looked mean, sipped tea from his whiskey bottle, and stared at the proceedings. When Belissari turned around, he almost gasped. The horse was a pinto.

At Pete's reaction, Hardee smiled. "All right, McBride. The horse is ten yards in front of you. Do your magic."

Happy Jack McBride cautiously approached the horse, feeling his way with outstretched arms that finally pressed against the gelding's white face. Pete held his breath as McBride rubbed the animal. It was an ugly horse, only eleven hands, with a white mane and forelegs. Happy worked his hands like a master potter, spreading his fingers across the brown and white hair. The side of the horse's face was brown, as were its ears, and there were brown markings on its sides and back, along with a brown left rear leg. Pete looked for a reaction from McBride as his hands moved from white to brown, but the blind man revealed nothing.

Two minutes passed with no sounds except from the livestock. Five minutes. Hardee shook his head and pulled out a pocket watch that chimed for a half second until he snapped the cover shut, returned it to his pocket, and stared at Belissari.

"I'm a busy man, Pete Belissari. Don't waste my time."

Happy Jack finally smiled and patted the horse's neck. "Ain't much of a horse you got here, Señor Hardee," he said. "Gelding. About fifteen years old. Got cracked heels and grass sickness. Needs a better diet when you get back to Fort Leaton. Can't say this nag is worth much. Might bring you a few dollars from the glue factory in El Paso."

"The color, mister. Just tell me the color."

Pete bit his lip.

"It's a skewbald," Happy Jack answered. Pete sighed and smiled. "Mostly white. Brown markings. That's a good trick, bringing in a pinto."

Hardee let out a cannonade of oaths, caught his breath, and cursed some more. He turned savagely at Belissari and yelled: "It's a dirty trick!"

"There's no trick to it," Pete replied, trying to keep his cool. "You want to bring in another horse, do it. Pick any from the corral, or one of your—"

Hardee was already moving. He ordered one of his riders to dismount, then pulled the Mexican's lathered mare toward Happy Jack, who shrugged and rubbed the horse for a couple of minutes before declaring, "Dapple gray."

Hardee cursed on his way to the corral, roped a blue roan, and stormed his way back into the yard. Two minutes later, after Happy Jack correctly guessed the color, the old scalphunter shrieked at another rider, who dropped from the saddle and led his gelding to the blind man.

"Strawberry roan," Happy Jack said after a brief examination. "Nice horse."

Cash Hardee was almost out of breath. He looked around—maybe for another horse, a piebald this time or an odd-colored pinto—then reached for one of his Tiffany Colts. "This is some trick, Belissari," he said in a hoarse whisper, "and I'll kill you for it."

At that moment, David Goldman stood up, scraping his chair against the porch floor. One of the Mexican gunmen whispered a prayer in Spanish; Hardee froze with his right hand just inches from his gun butt. Everyone in the yard was looking cautiously at the black-hatted gent who had been introduced as the legendary gunman Sabine Savage.

Hardee's hand inched away from his Colt. He looked at Belissari, who forced a smile and said, "There's no trick, Hardee. You can bring in a herd of horses and Happy Jack will get the color right. Now, you want to pay off your bet, or do you want to die here this morning?"

"Tomás!" Hardee yelled, then barked out an order in Spanish. A curly-haired gunman with a thin mustache dropped a leather pouch at Belissari's feet and backed away.

"You win this time, Pete Belissari, but this isn't finished," Hardee said.

"No," Pete said. "It's not. We still have business to do. I need horses for this stage line."

"Huh?"

"Horses. I still need to buy stock."

The scalphunter's scarred forehead wrinkled in confusion.

"From you." Pete had never considered himself a salesman until now. He still needed Cash Hardee—his livestock anyway—so he had to take the sting out of the killer's loss. That shouldn't be too hard, he hoped. He was basically giving Hardee a chance to recoup his gambling losses. "Now that we've got these fun and games over with," Pete continued, "maybe we can just sit down, have breakfast, and do business."

Slowly Hardee nodded. "Buddy," Belissari said, "show Mr. Hardee and Happy Jack inside." He turned to Hardee's riders. "You men, tend to your animals. Help yourselves to water. Coffee will be ready in ten minutes." He repeated his words in Spanish, then, finally breathing easier, walked to the shack where David Goldman stood frozen, eyes squinting, looking indeed like some hero on a dime-novel cover.

Pete stopped on the porch and smiled at Goldman. He glanced inside, made sure Hardee wasn't eavesdropping and said softly, "Standing up like that, Dave. That was brilliant. You probably stopped a shooting match."

"B-b-brilliant?" Goldy's face was drained of any color, and this close, he looked like some jester rather than a feared gunman.

"Yeah," Pete said in a whisper. "Standing up took the fight out of them. Are you all right?"

The large black Stetson swayed stupidly as Goldman shook his head. "Pete," he said, "I only stood up because I had to go to the privy. I been drinking tea all mornin'."

Chapter Seven

Winter refused to yield on Valentine's Day, buffeting the Davis Mountains with a biting wind that caused the old timbers in Hannah's cabin to creak and moan. A hard freeze left the ground crusted white with frost, and the gray clouds to the west threatened snow.

Hannah Scott was glad to be inside, where the children worked their math problems as she studied the map Pete had tacked up on the wall. Outside, Pete and Buddy Pecos were repairing the old stagecoach while Irwin and Everhart finished the roof on the patio.

Pecos had marked each station on the map. North from Presidio, the first stop was in Shafter, run by two men named McBride and Goldman. Two other swing stations were marked at Cienega and Perdiz creeks before reaching a home station in Marfa at the Marfa Hotel. The next stop was at Fort Davis, run by Lempert's Addition and R. Van Boskirk's livery, then on to Hannah's swing station. After another stop at Ezra Boone's ranch, the stage would pull into Barrilla Springs, a raw, lawless post with a reputation for violence that went back thirty years.

Hannah thought Everhart could have picked a better place for a home station.

After Barrilla Springs, the map was marked with two more swing stations, at W. J. Stewart's ranch and

Dusty Cleburne's trading post, before reaching the final stop at Fort Stockton. On the map, the route looked easy, but Hannah had traveled enough across the mountains and desert to know it could be a windmilling ride from Presidio to Fort Stockton.

Oldenburgs and American geldings pranced in the new corral, and Pete had stocked all of the stations south of Fort Davis with strong horses that he bought from Cash Hardee. The stations from Hannah's ranch to Fort Stockton were also ready. Everhart had contracts with each station master, although only two—Hannah's and the one at Shafter Station—were exclusive. All of the other stations could also be leased by other outfits, including the new Coffey and Co.

She heard the squeaking wheel despite the wind and stepped outside as the sparkling Phaeton, drawn by two black horses, pulled into the yard. Hannah regretted not putting on a coat but decided against going back inside. The buggy was shiny black with a gold stripe, brass lanterns on each side, and a black leather top. The gear was painted green, matching the tufted seats. A rig like that, she thought, must belong to a banker, which is why she stopped suddenly when a beautiful woman with auburn hair was helped down by the driver.

The driver was a chinless gunman . . . Tubac.

The men had stopped working and approached the visitors, with the exception of Irwin, who must have recognized Tubac and was leaning against the smaller corral with Pete's Winchester in his arms.

''Miss Coffey,'' Everhart said.

The woman smiled as she adjusted the pin in her newly curled hair. She held a square package under her left arm. "Mr. Everhart," she greeted. "Mr. Pecos. Pete. It's good to see you."

Pete! That was awfully familiar. Hannah's gaze hardened and fastened on her beau. He pushed back his hat and smiled politely, but Hannah caught him glancing her way. She trusted Pete, but he would not hear the end of this for a month.

"There was a package waiting for you at the mercantile," Jill Coffey told Pete, "and I took the liberty of bringing it out to you."

Pete stepped forward and took the package, thanking her and stepping back. "It's cold out here," he said. "Would y'all like to go inside?"

"I don't think so," she said, nodding at Tubac, who pulled an envelope from the inside pocket of his mackinaw and handed it to a frowning Dean Everhart.

"This is a letter from the postmaster. It seems he hasn't awarded you—or me—a mail contract yet. What he proposes is that we run a race, from Fort Stockton to Presidio. The stagecoach line with the fastest time will get the mail contract."

Pete, Pecos, and Hannah gathered around Everhart as he ripped open the envelope and devoured the words. It was just as Coffey stated. The woman waited patiently for a response.

"And you're game for this race, Miss Coffey?" Everhart finally asked.

"I was born game," the gambler replied with a laugh.

"How do you propose we run this race?" This time it was Buddy Pecos who spoke.

Coffey shrugged. "We meet in Fort Stockton next Monday. That gives us a week. One of us leaves Tuesday at a certain time, say, early or midmorning. The next day the second stage leaves. The fastest coach wins the contract, and probably stays in business. Without a mail contract, I don't think you could keep your head above water.''

Everhart nodded.

''Who keeps the time?'' Hannah asked.

Jill studied her for a minute. She glanced at Pete, then back at Hannah, and finally smiled. ''Sheriff Slaughter will oversee the contest. That will keep us all honest. We'll have judges in Presidio, Marfa, Fort Davis, and Fort Stockton.''

The men were nodding now. Then Jill said, ''Or I could just buy you out, make things easier on us all.''

Instantly Pecos, Pete, and Everhart started shaking their heads, mumbling nos and can't dos and no thank yous. But Hannah asked, ''What's your offer?''

Coffey shrugged, smiled coyly, and replied, ''Five hundred dollars.''

Now Hannah scoffed. ''That's not an offer. That's an insult.''

''Yes,'' Coffey replied, ''it is. But it beats losing everything. I'll make it six hundred, but that's it. Take it or leave it.''

Hannah forgot about hospitality. Her face flushed. ''We'll leave it,'' she snapped, ''and you please leave.''

The woman smiled again, nodded at Tubac, and climbed into the buggy. ''Then I'll see y'all in Fort Stockton next week. Good luck. This should be much more enjoyable than cards.''

As soon as the buggy was out of sight, Hannah led her partners and Irwin Sawyer inside the cabin, pouring each a cup of coffee, then turning her attention to the children. "Christopher," she said, "I want you to grade the math problems. The rest of you, tend your chores."

"Who were those folks, Mama Hannah?" Angelica asked.

"Just some people from town," she replied. "Now hurry along."

"What did that woman give you, Pete?" Paco asked, ignoring Hannah's orders.

"That ain't no woman, kiddo," Everhart said. "That's Jill Coffey."

Hannah cringed. Paco shrieked. "*The* Jill Coffey? The Black Widow? Gosh a-mighty, why didn't y'all bring her in? I really wanted to meet her."

"Paco," Hannah pleaded.

"But, Mama Hannah, you know I like them Black Widow books. It just ain't fair!"

"Paco! Your chores!"

Cynthia grabbed the boy's arm and led him outside. Hannah glared at Everhart for mentioning Coffey's name. What an idiot! She controlled her temper, took a deep breath, and tried to relax. Pete was sitting at the table, opening his package. He pulled out a pair of black leather boots, eighteen inches high with square toes and Cuban heels.

"Mighty pretty," Pecos said.

"Yeah," Pete said. He looked at Hannah and smiled. "Thank you, kindly."

Everhart cleared his throat. "All right, now that we got that out of the way, we need to start thinking about this fine pickle. If we don't get that mail contract, we are dead."

''Well, it ain't my business,'' a voice drawled, and everyone turned to face Irwin, still cradling the Winchester, except Pete. ''Anyway, this here Jill Coffey ain't got no stagecoachin' experience and all, and y'all do. That should mean y'all should win that race.''

A hard frown creased Pete's face. He seldom, if ever, even spoke to the cowhand, and Irwin did as much as he could to stay out of the horseman's way. The two tolerated each other, but only because of Hannah. She wished the two could be friends, but she understood Pete's jealousy. She would be glad when Irwin finished his work and went back to Julian Cale's ranch.

Pecos nodded. ''Should. But lots of things can happen. Rain could wash out a road. Axle could break.''

Pete placed his boots on the floor. ''Jill Coffey says she plays to win,'' he said. He stared ahead at the map on the wall.

''Meaning?'' Everhart asked, but Pete only shrugged.

As far as Hannah knew, Coffey and Co. had no contracts with any stations between Presidio and Fort Stockton. She could get them easy enough, except at Shafter and this place, but there were other places willing to lease buildings, land, and livestock. Coffey owned only one stagecoach; so did their company. Irwin was right. Buddy and Everhart had experience with stagecoaching, Pete knew horses and the area, but in a race across almost two hundred miles, luck would be a big factor.

''First thing we need to do,'' Everhart said, ''is get the coach to Fort Stockton. Buddy, I think you should light out with Pete, get a feel for everything. I'll head down to Presidio, get things organized.''

''And me?'' Hannah asked.

''You and Irwin just stay here, finish up things. Not much else you can do.''

She awoke with a start, wondering if she had been dreaming, listening in the darkness. The wind screamed outside as the norther blew in, but above that, she could hear something outside. Horses snorting. And something else. Hannah wished Pete were here, but he and Pecos had left that afternoon for Fort Stockton. Everhart had gone to Presidio, but Irwin was close—she hoped.

Hannah sat up, slid her feet into the felt slippers at her bedside, and pulled a greatcoat over her wool undervest and drawers. First she checked on the children, but all five were fast asleep on their cots, then she found the .38-caliber Colt Lightning she kept above the door, out of the children's reach. She lifted the latch and stepped outside, pulling the door shut behind her.

The wind took her breath away. The temperature had dropped at least thirty degrees in a matter of hours, and it had been cold to begin with. Clouds obscured the moon and stars, but as her eyes adjusted to the darkness, she noticed movement by the corral, and the wind carried the muffled cries of horses . . . and curses of men.

Where is Irwin? she thought. The cowboy had been bunking in the barn, but she couldn't wait, couldn't look for him. Men were stealing her Oldenburgs. She could make out the forms of several men in front of her, knocking down the corral rails, trying to round up the herd of horses already spooked by the weather. Slowly she crept forward, gun barrel pointed ahead, the trigger guard cold against her finger. Hannah tried to swallow, but couldn't, then pulled back the hammer of the Colt even though the revolver was double-action so that she only had to squeeze the trigger to fire.

Horses screamed as a rider rode into the corral, yelling and raising something in his hand—Hannah thought it was a lariat—over his head. She raised her arm and was about to yell at the intruders to halt, when she spotted a motion to her left. Hannah turned, gasping as she swung the Colt around, felt something crash against her temple, and heard the deafening roar of her pistol.

Orange and red flashes exploded in front of her eyes, though they were shut tightly, each time her heart beat. She knew she lay flat on the ground, heard the screams of men and animals and the pounding of hooves that grew fainter. A door opened. Christopher called out her name, and she tried to respond but her mouth wouldn't work. Finally, she struggled to a sitting position. The wind blew open her coat and chilled her.

"Mama Hannah!" Chris was at her side now, his face panic-stricken as she regained her vision. "You're bleeding!" She nodded tentatively, felt the blood running down her cheek, and turned toward the big corral. The Oldenburgs and other horses for the stagecoach were gone, though the thieves had left behind the saddle horses, including Duck Pegasus and Lightning Flash. That was stupid, she thought.

"I'm all right," she told Chris. "Find Irwin."

She pulled herself to her knees, buttoned the coat, and tried to stand. The world suddenly went spinning out of control; Hannah felt nauseated and then fell into a deep, black well.

Chapter Eight

Barrilla Springs Station was as forlorn a place as Pete had ever seen: crumbling adobe walls repeatedly whipped by a hard wind, a rundown corral and outer buildings, and a graveyard that was twice the size of the stagecoach station. "Unknown" declared many of the wooden crosses; quite a few proclaimed the epitaph "Murdered"; some were marked only with a stick, rock, or nothing at all. The cemetery didn't even contain the numerous Federal soldiers killed by Indians and assorted riffraff near, and sometimes inside, the station. The soldiers were buried at Forts Davis and Stockton.

Three times the main building had been destroyed only to be rebuilt: by Apaches during the early '60s, after a violent shootout in '74, and by a mysterious fire in '80. The two stationmasters, Hopkins and Griggs, were unreconstructed Rebels, so strong in their Southern sympathies that they would make Buddy Pecos look like a Unionist. They attracted other old Confederates, who constantly tormented and provoked the Union troops assigned to guard duty at the station. Five years earlier, with tensions boiling between the station hands and Army detail, the station burned. More than a few people thought the soldiers started the blaze, and Belissari couldn't blame them.

No soldiers were at Barrilla Springs when Pete and Pecos parked the old Concord at dusk and unhitched the team. With the Apaches subdued, the Army saw no need in guarding the outpost, and the last regular stage line had ceased operations in '82. But Barrilla Springs still attracted a crowd, offering travelers a place to drink and eat, play cards and sleep, and, if they weren't careful, die.

Inside, Pecos and Belissari stood beside the Duke Cannon stove, warming themselves while Griggs filled two tin mugs with coffee, then sprayed the side of the stove with tobacco juice, which sizzled against the sheet-iron drum. Pecos shifted his Sharps underneath his left arm and took one cup. Griggs handed the other to Belissari, who took a sip and nodded politely. The coffee was awful.

Griggs was as solid as an oak keg, with green eyes and thinning gray-red hair. He wore a week's growth of beard, brown canvas pants, scuffed boots, and a dirty muslin shirt that hadn't been washed since the last rain. Come to think of it, Belissari thought, Horace Griggs probably hadn't bathed since spring.

His partner, Luke Hopkins, leaned in a wooden chair in the far corner, head tilted back against the wall, eyes closed and mouth open, snoring loudly. Hopkins had black hair, streaked with silver, grease, and grime, and a thick silver mustache. A Parker shotgun rested on his lap, both hammers pulled back.

Five other men were inside. Four sat at a corner table, obscured by thick cigar smoke and dim lighting as they dealt cards and drank whiskey. The fifth man was Sheriff Slick Slaughter, who stood in the back holding a pool stick beside a huge, green billiard table.

How Hopkins and Griggs ever got that through the door would always be a mystery.

''Peter, my boy,'' Slaughter said. ''How about joining me in a game?''

Belissari wasn't much at billiards, but he decided it would be a good way to kill the time, or at least escape the stove's stifling heat, which was almost putting him to sleep. He didn't see how Pecos and Griggs could stand it that hot, so he took his coffee cup and found a cue stick that wasn't too warped.

''What brings you out this way, Sheriff?'' Pete asked after Slaughter dropped one ball in a side pocket on the break, and sank three consecutive shots before missing.

''Business,'' Slaughter replied and left it at that.

Pete lost the first game, and racked the balls for another.

''You boys ready for your stagecoach race?'' Slaughter asked, casually wiping the lenses of his glasses with a bandanna.

Shrugging, Pete found some chalk in the corner and rubbed down his stick. ''Seems strange,'' he finally said, ''that the postmaster would let a race decide a mail contract rather than award it to a company with experience in the business.''

Slaughter laughed. ''Peter, you don't have a lick of experience with stage lines, nor does sweet little Miss Hannah. And I don't know what alley ex-Sheriff Pecos found Everhart in, but . . .'' He bent over the table, aimed, and sent the cue ball rifling over the green cloth, striking the racked balls and sending the twelve ball into the left corner pocket.

''I'm on a roll,'' Slaughter said triumphantly. All

through the game, he needled Pete about the Everhart-Pecos-Belissari-Scott stage. He doubted if that coach could haul a flea from here to Leon Springs. He wondered if Buddy Pecos could see well enough to drive with only one eye. He wondered if Hannah would be "entertaining" the passengers at Old Man Iverson's former ranch.

Pete straightened at the last remark. "Back up, Sheriff," he said coldly.

"Boy," Slaughter replied, "you just concentrate on making that bank shot. When you miss, I'll show you how it's done." He smiled proudly. "I'm not Greek. I'm a Texan, born and breed. My Uncle Thaddeus died at the Alamo."

Belissari was a native Texan too, though his parents were born in Greece. He snorted at Slaughter's comment on the Alamo, though. The sheriff was picking a fight. Belissari knew this, and he was ready to accommodate him.

"You got a problem, Peter?" Slaughter asked. "You calling me a liar about Uncle Thaddeus?"

"Nope," Pete said. "I'm sure your uncle was at the Alamo. Along with a bunch of other yacks who disobeyed Sam Houston's orders and got what they deserved."

The station went suddenly quiet. Belissari hadn't meant for his voice to carry as far as it did, but now he heard only Hopkins's snores and the wood burning in the stove. A chair leg scraped against the floor. Slick Slaughter put his pool stick in the rack and found his coat.

"Well," he said. "I need to get back to the office. Thanks for the game, Peter, my boy." Slaughter nodded at Griggs and Pecos, found his hat by the door, and stepped into the cold night. Belissari stared at the four men who had been playing cards. One was nearly the size of a cow, two were dressed in greasy leather buckskins and smelled of buffalo guts, and the fourth cracked his knuckles and smiled a toothless grin.

"What was that you said 'bout the Alamo, boy?" Toothless asked.

Still holding his pool stick, Belissari unbuckled his gun belt and tossed it on the table. Slaughter had set him up, leaving him to these four wolves and conveniently disappearing before the fight, which, as sheriff, he would be compelled to break up. Pete watched as the four rapscallions unfastened their hardware—revolvers, knives, even a pair of brass knuckles—and tossed them onto the table. Buddy Pecos stood silently by the stove, sipping coffee, ignoring Belissari's plight. Well, it was Pete's fight, and Pecos might have taken offense at the Alamo insult.

"All right, big mouth," Toothless continued. "Fists it'll be."

Pete brought up the pool stick and swung it as hard as he could, breaking it across Toothless's head.

Roland Kibbee's adobe hut lay in the aptly named Horse Thief Canyon at the base of a hill covered with scrub brush, small trees, and dark lava rocks. Hannah stared past the abysmal shack and at the Oldenburgs and other livestock eating hay in the solid corral. Kibbee pranced excitedly around his place, looking intently toward the southwest before disappearing inside the trading post.

"He's waitin' for somebody," Irwin Sawyer whispered.

Julian Cale grunted. "He doesn't want to keep that stock longer than he has to. Likely has someone lined up to buy them and get them out of the country. Probably running late. Expect he wanted to get rid of those horses first thing this morning."

Hannah's head hurt, but she had insisted on riding with Cale and Irwin to Kibbee's place and she wasn't about to let on. After the raid, Christopher had found Irwin unconscious and hog-tied in the barn. The teen had helped Irwin and Hannah inside, then mounted Lightning Flash and ridden to Julian Cale's ranch. Cale returned with five cowboys and a half-breed tracker named Leopold. At dawn, they took off after the horses, leaving one cowboy behind at Hannah's place for the children's sake. Hannah insisted on coming with them, much to Cale's and Irwin's displeasure.

Leopold led the posse straight to Roland Kibbee's, took his payment—a dollar and a bottle of Milton Faver's famous peach brandy—and rode toward Fort Davis. That had been a waste of money, Hannah thought. The first place she would have looked for stolen horses would have been Kibbee's Trading Post.

Roland Kibbee was a vile man with thick, red hair and a pale face. For years, he had run a miserable trading post, dealing bad whiskey to anyone with a dime, and buying and selling stolen horses. Before that, some said, he had been a Comanchero, trading guns and anything else to Plains Indians. Folks called him "Maggot."

Cale stood and said, "Miss Scott, stay here with

Irwin. The rest of us are riding down there to pay Maggot a visit.''

Hannah shook her head. ''I'm going with you.''

''Miss Scott, I let you come this far. But no farther. I'll motion for you to join us when we have Maggot. That shouldn't take long.''

''I'm going,'' Hannah said.

''Ma'am,'' Cale said, with a sudden fierceness in his voice that Hannah had never heard, ''I ain't never had a woman killed, and I won't risk that now. You are staying put!''

The five men pounded down the hill as Hannah and Irwin watched from the safety of the trees. She saw Kibbee step outside, heard him shriek like a pig as he ran toward the corral. There was the puff of white smoke from Cale's rifle, followed by the loud report that echoed down the canyon. Kibbee fell backward, then took off away from the cabin. One of the riders cut him off on horseback as easily as he would have a cow during roundup. The horse thief stumbled and crawled several yards before finding his feet and sprinting again.

A bullet whined off a rock. Kibbee screamed. A lariat looped over the man's chest and tightened, and Maggot yelped as he was jerked hard to the ground. The cowboy quickly wrapped his rope around the saddle horn three times, turned his gelding, and dragged Roland Kibbee back to his shack.

Maggot was crying by the time Hannah and Irwin rode to the post. Cale had led Kibbee inside, tied his hands behind his back with pigging string and towered above him as his cowhands helped themselves to the trader's whiskey and tobacco.

''Where did you get those horses, Maggot?'' Cale boomed.

''I-I-I bought them off'n a feller named . . . Smith. I gots a bill of sale—''

Cale slapped him with a gloved right hand. ''Don't play me for a fool, Maggot.''

Kibbee sobbed. ''I swear, mister, I ain't—''

Hannah shuddered at the second slap. Blood trickled from Kibbee's nose and over his trembling lips. ''I . . . I swear the man said his name was Smith. I ain't never seen him before. It's the gospel truth, and I'll swear on a stack of bibles.''

''Who you plan on selling them to?''

''Uh . . . uh.'' Kibbee flinched as Cale raised his hand again, but this time the rancher didn't slap him.

''Maggot, you disgust me,'' Cale said, lowering his arm. ''You're a liar and a thief, and I, for one, am sick of it. You knew these Oldenburgs were stolen—''

''I swear I didn't.''

With one hand, Cale lifted the man out of his seat and flung him across the bar, a one-by-eight-inch board nailed to two old pickle barrels. He grabbed a handful of red hair and jerked Kibbee back into his chair, which would have toppled backward if a black cowboy with a silver mustache and goatee had not stopped it with his right foot.

''Six of those horses in your corral are Oldenburgs, you *lépero,*'' Cale said. The rancher's eyes were menacing, his breath short. ''Everyone in Presidio County knows that those are my horses. Were my horses, anyway. Now they're Miss Scott's. And from what I've heard, you have tormented her before. Well, Maggot, it's over now.''

Julian Cale turned toward the tallest cowboy, a lanky man with sandy hair and a walrus mustache. ''Dillon,'' he said, ''get a rope.''

Chapter Nine

"Nice fight," Buddy Pecos said as Belissari washed his face in the water trough the next morning. Pete grunted something, gently touching the knot on his forehead, cut under his right eye, and swollen lips. Pecos didn't look a whole lot better, but his face was so scarred it was hard to notice the new splotches, bruises, and cuts.

Slowly, unsteadily, Belissari followed Pecos to the Concord. The lanky gunman shoved his Sharps onto the roof, then pulled himself into the driver's box. Pete tried to climb up beside him, but had to be helped by Pecos, who released the brake and smiled as the mustanger got settled.

"Nice fight," a voice drawled, and Pete opened his eyes and looked below. Horace Griggs spit out a mouthful of tobacco juice and grinned. Pete wasn't sure if his eyes were playing tricks on him or not, but it looked as if the stationmaster's left earlobe had been bitten off. Griggs worked on the tobacco with his teeth, looked at Pecos, and said, "So, we'll see you next week sometime."

Buddy nodded. "Might make a run back to Fort Davis before then. Try not to have Jill Coffey's welcoming committee waiting for us next time, Griggs."

The man laughed. "Pecos, an old Johnny Reb like

you can take care of anything some petticoat gambler dishes out to you. Y'all proved that last night. We'll be ready for you, but Coffey and Co. is paying us too. We gotta help them, also, but me and Luke will be rootin' for you.''

Pete didn't really understand what they were talking about. He had a headache, was sore all over, and felt like he had been trampled by buffalo. He looked at the team of horses in front of him, saw Luke Hopkins fastening the last harness. Hopkins stepped to the side, smiled at Belissari, and said, ''You boys are all set. Have a good trip.''

Hopkins's right eye was black and blue and swollen shut.

Pecos unleashed a stream of oaths and whipped the reins. The stagecoach jumped forward, Belissari groaned, and they left Barrilla Springs. ''Good luck, gents!'' Hopkins yelled as the stagecoach pulled onto the road.

As Pecos concentrated on driving, Pete tried to piece together what had happened that night.

Toothless had dropped to the floor when Belissari broke the pool stick over his head. He jabbed the blunt end of the remaining piece into the dark-haired buckskinner's stomach, who doubled over as Pete brought up his knee and busted the man's nose. The other man in buckskins, with a crooked beak for a nose, grabbed Pete from behind, pinning his arms, and the fat man smiled and stepped closer, but Pete brought up his legs and buried his brand-new boots into Fatty's gut, then slammed the boot heels on Crooked Nose's feet. Belissari broke free, spun around, and threw a left that sent Crooked Nose sailing over the pool table. Pete turned in time to see Fatty's fist, about the size of a ham, heading toward his face. The blow catapulted Belissari into the rack of pool sticks, and he crashed to the floor.

Things got a bit hazy after that.

Buddy Pecos laughed when asked to fill in the details. He flipped the reins, washed the side of the coach with tobacco juice, and shouted over the squeaking Concord and pounding hooves.

"As soon as you decked that *hombre* with the pool stick, I slammed the butt of my Sharps into Griggs's belly!"

"Griggs? Why?"

"To keep him from gettin' any ideas. I've knowed Horace for ten years. He'd just as soon fight as eat. 'Bout that time, Hopkins was comin' wide awake, raising that scattergun, so I hefted up my rifle and shot a leg off'n his chair. He crashed to the floor, blasted both barrels into the ceiling and a pretty big chunk of rock caught him under the eye, knocked him out cold."

Belissari shook his head. He vaguely remembered the loud gunshots, the smell of powder. But by then, he had his hands full with the three ruffians still conscious.

"Anyway," Pecos continued, "I put the Big Fifty in a safe place, then pulled that fat cuss off'n you and laid him out with the butt of my Schofield. Unfortunately, I didn't hit Griggs hard enough and he popped me upside the head with an empty coffeepot."

He paused long enough to curse the lead horses, lashed out at them with his whip, then went on: "One of them skinners, though, punched Griggs in the jaw, and ol' Horace got him in a headlock and rammed him several times against that hot stove. Man, that burnin' hair sure does stink. I flung the Schofield on the pool table, it bein' a fistfight and all, and jumped on that fella you knocked out who was wakin' up and about to throw the cue ball at you. That other skinner saw what Griggs was doin', so he left off beatin' the tarnation out of you and went to help his pard, but Hopkins had woke up too, and he knocked that cuss's teeth out with his chair.

"Then that big fella got up, grabbed Hopkins and Griggs, and knocked their heads together. Next thing I know, you is yellin' like a Reb, come flyin' across the room and kick that guy in the chest and send him crashin' through the door." He spit again, wiped his lips with a shirtsleeve, and nodded, satisfied. "Knocked the door clean off its hinges."

"And?"

"And?" Pecos laughed. "That was it, Pete. Least, that's all I recall."

"What happened to Griggs's ear?"

Pecos only shrugged, whipped the reins again, and shook his head, reveling in the memory. "Yes sir," he said, "it was one Jim Dandy fight."

They rode on to the next swing station, had a quick cup of coffee while the stockmen changed the team and greased the rear axle, then reboarded the Concord and continued the journey to Fort Stockton.

Pete was asleep about an hour later when Pecos nudged him and said, "Here, you give it a whirl."

Belissari blinked groggily as his friend offered him the heavy reins. In an instant, he came wide awake. "You fool! I can't handle a team."

"It's time you learned. Take off them gloves first, though."

Pete protested. It was freezing, and the wind had already numbed his hands despite the heavy gloves. But Pecos wasn't wearing gloves. "Do it," the gunman ordered; Pete complied and took the reins. They were heavy, jerking his arms every which way for several seconds until he gained some semblance of control. The horses proceeded at a canter.

Buddy Pecos laughed. "You don't wear gloves when you're a jehu," he said. "Interferes with the touch. This job takes a steady hand, good feel. Cold is a problem. I recall a fella named Martin Jarrett on the run from Boggy Depot to Colbert's Ferry in the Nations. Blue norther blew in one January, he got a bad case of frostbite and was knowed as Three Fingers Jarrett afterwards."

The former sharpshooter reached down and took the three pairs of reins, wrapping them through the fingers in Pete's left hand. "Takes some gettin' used to," Pecos said and pointed to one set of reins. "Them's for the leaders." Another set. "Them's the middle pair." He tapped the final two reins. "Them's the wheelers." Pecos lifted the whip and handed it to Belissari, who took it with his right, free, hand.

"Mostly, the horses act as a team, but you can control each pair separately, 'specially in turns and such. You can use both hands, but I use my left for the reins and right for the whip. 'Course, when we're flyin', it's best to use both hands on the reins. Good jehu can pick a fly off'n a horse's tail with a whip. You ain't never drove a rig?"

Pete shook his head and stared at the road. He was

afraid he'd run off and wreck. He had driven jerkies and buckboards, and back in college had earned extra cash by driving a milk wagon, but those were only one- or two-horse wagons. Not six. And nothing going this fast.

"You got the knack, Pete," Pecos said. "I figured that, knowin' horses like you do. Give me a few days, and you'll be a regular jehu. Now I'm gonna get me some shut-eye."

Pecos was snoring in seconds, but he jerked awake ten minutes later when Pete pulled back on the reins and set the brake, yelling, "Whoa! Whoa!"

"What's the matter?" Pecos blinked as Pete pointed at the road. Sitting in the middle of the path was a dog, a dark mongrel with floppy black ears and protruding bones, panting. Slowly it sat up and began wagging its tail.

Buddy Pecos scowled at Pete, who shrugged. "He wouldn't get out of the way," Pete explained. "I yelled. But I couldn't just run over him."

The dog barked happily.

"I could," Pecos said.

Hannah gasped when two of the cowhands stood Kibbee on the chair while another tossed a lariat over a rafter, secured one end, and tightened the loop over Maggot's neck. The horse thief was sobbing uncontrollably now.

"Ain't none of us knows how to make a hangman's noose, Mr. Cale," the man called Dillon said.

The rancher swore vehemently and shouted, "This isn't Nathan Hale we're hanging! It's Maggot! He doesn't deserve a proper noose."

Kibbee caught his breath between sobs and pleaded. "You . . . t-thi-this . . . ain't right . . . Mr. Cale. We . . . we . . . we got laws."

"Tyler Slaughter?" Cale snorted.

"But . . . y-you . . . ca-can't do this."

"I can and I will, Maggot! I hanged the Defarge brothers in '73, and I'm going to hang you."

At first, Hannah thought Cale was bluffing, trying to scare Kibbee into naming his accomplices. But the look on the rancher's face, the brutality in his voice, told her he would lynch the man without regret. His eyes were void of compassion. A couple of Cale's hired hands, including Irwin, stared at their boots, uncomfortable with this act of . . . well, it was murder, plain and simple. But none would stand up to his boss. Dillon and the black cowboy stood casually. Another watched excitedly as if he were at a Shakespeare play.

Hannah's stomach turned. She had seen enough violence in her life: beatings, gunfights, men killed. But this was totally different, and when Cale told Kibbee that he had half a minute to say his prayers, she knew she would not, could not, be a part of this.

"Mr. Cale," she said, stepping forward. The rancher turned on her savagely. She cleared her throat, took a breath, and said as forcefully as she could under his malevolent glare, "You can't do this. It's murder."

"Step outside, Miss Scott, if you don't want to watch. I knew I shouldn't have let you come along."

"No," she said. Hannah detested Roland Kibbee, hated protecting him now, but she could not live with herself if she allowed this to happen.

"Dillon," Cale said. "Get her out of my sight."

The cowboy looked uncomfortably at his boss, then

took a step toward her, mumbling an apology, but Hannah backed up and said, ''If you lynch him, Cale, I'll see you hanged for murder. All of you.''

The cowboy stopped. Cale's eyes locked intensely on Hannah, but she refused to cower or look away. A minute passed. The rancher finally blinked, grunted something, and turned to the black cowboy. ''Cut him down, Striker,'' he said. ''Sawyer. You stay with me. The rest of you boys, get those stolen horses back to Miss Scott's ranch.''

Kibbee, with his hands still bound behind him, dropped at Hannah's feet and leaned against her, sobbing like a baby, blubbering out thanks. Hannah backed away from him, disgusted at his filth, and Cale lifted him with his good hand and threw him against the wall.

''You're a lucky man, Maggot,'' Cale said. ''But I'm not done with you yet. Now who sold you those horses?''

Maggot caught his breath and asked for a glass of whiskey. Cale relented, and Irwin poured him a mug that he drank down like tea. ''I swear, Mr. Cale, I ain't never seen the man before. He just rode in last night past midnight with the horses and some other men, said I was buyin' them horses and that someone would be over this morn to buy them from me and get them out of the country. I knowed they was your Oldenburgs, but this man made me buy 'em. That's the truth, Mr. Cale.''

Cale spit on the floor. ''What did he look like?''

''I don't know.''

''Maggot!''

"Just a regular fella. Dark hair. Carried a big old Winchester. First time I had ever seen him."

Hannah stepped forward. "Did he have a chin?" She didn't really know why she asked. It was a long shot. Kibbee stared at her blankly. Outside, Cale's cowboys were herding the horses out of the canyon and back toward her ranch. Finally, Kibbee answered.

"He had a beard. Wore a black Stetson Boss of the Plains. That's about all I recollect."

It wasn't Tubac. Hannah nodded. *Well, at least we have the horses back,* she thought. Cale battered Kibbee with questions for fifteen more minutes but got nothing else from the trader. Hannah was convinced that he was telling the truth.

"All right, Maggot," Cale said. "I'm letting you go with your life. Get out of Texas. If I ever see you again, I'll kill you on sight."

"But what about my place here?"

"You won't have a place in half an hour. I'm going to burn it. Now get."

Maggot scrambled out of the door. Cale told Irwin to splash the walls and floors with coal oil or Kibbee's whiskey, and as the cowboy carried out his orders, the rancher stared at Hannah. Outside, Kibbee cursed his mule.

"You're too soft for this way of life, Miss Scott," Cale said without malice.

"There are those who would disagree with you."

"You should have let me hang Maggot. He deserved it."

Hannah shook her head. "That's wrong, Mr. Cale. You're running him out of this state. That's enough."

"Your beau tried to run him out last year. He came back."

She smiled, though it was forced. "He won't come back this time. Not with you as my neighbor."

Cale swore under his breath, shook his head, and mumbled something that sounded like "Maybe I'm the one too soft for this country." He told Irwin to splash the roof with the rest of the coal oil, then tear down the corral and lean-to. Once the fire was out, they would pull down the adobe walls with ropes on horseback.

Hannah followed the two men outside. She was walking toward her horse when she heard the gunshot and Julian Cale's scream.

Chapter Ten

Julian Cale's face had turned white, and he grimaced and fell back against the shack, hopping on his left leg as blood poured through two wicked holes in his right foot. Hannah gasped, then screamed as a bullet disintegrated the old bucket by the well in Kibbee's yard. Almost immediately, a third shot slammed into the adobe wall, just inches from Cale's head. Groaning, the rancher fell inside the doorway and crawled to safety.

A bullet zipped past Hannah's ear, then she felt a crushing blow as Irwin Sawyer tackled her and pushed her behind the well. She opened her eyes, cringed at another gunshot. Irwin sat up, crouching behind the limestone well, and chambered a round into his Winchester. Their terrified horses pulled at their tethers while Kibbee's two remaining horses and burro pounded through the corral gate the fleeing horse thief had left open.

One of the horses dropped in a heap as a gunshot echoed. The burro cried, turned, and barreled through the door into the trading post. Cale shouted fiercely, but his curses were soon lost amid the crashing of glass, tin, and wood inside the shack. By then, Kibbee's last horse sped down the canyon, somersaulted several times, and landed with an awful thud and lay still. Hannah wasn't sure if the animal had been shot or had stepped in a gopher hole.

Cale's horse, a beautiful strawberry roan, broke its tether, reared, and crashed against the corral as a rifle boomed. Blood spurted from the animal's head, and the two other mounts backed away, but Irwin was up and running, grabbing the reins, yelling, trying to pull the animals behind the cabin, out of the gunman's rifle sights. A bullet dug up sand at Sawyer's feet, and Hannah stood up, ready to help.

"Get down!" Irwin yelled. A bullet tore through Hannah's left shirtsleeve, and she fell in a panic, watching helplessly as Sawyer fought the terrified horses. His hat flew off. Two more shots echoed, and she heard a bullet strike flesh. Then Irwin disappeared behind the house as a final shot clipped the building's roof.

The echoes died. Even the cabin was silent. Kibbee's horse in front raised its head and cried out piteously. Hannah heard Cale's soft curse, then a pistol shot from inside the house, and the horse quivered and died.

"Irwin!" Hannah shouted.

"I'm all right!"

She sighed, but the cease-fire was short-lived. Six shots came from the hills furiously, one striking the well and the others slamming into the cabin's open doorway. The burro inside bellowed; Cale cursed and somehow managed to close the door. Another bullet thudded against the wooden door, and silence returned.

Hannah wiped sweat from her eyes. She was dying of thirst and only inches from water, but to raise her head risked death. The sharpshooter was somewhere up the canyon, armed with a heavy repeating rifle, for she had heard only one gun. At first she thought it had been Kibbee, but he rode out in the opposite direction and would not have shot his own horses. No, this was someone else. Maybe the man who had sold the stolen stock to Maggot. Maybe the buyer Kibbee had been waiting on. Or someone else.

"Sawyer!" Cale's voice cracked with pain. "Sawyer, those two horses all right?"

"Yes sir, Mr. Cale! One got nicked in her neck, but it ain't too bad!"

The noisy burro kicked the wall. Cale swore furiously, then all was lost in another round of steady fire. One bullet struck the well and sent a piece of rock, or perhaps lead, against Hannah's cheek. She buried her face in her hands and hugged the earth as the bullets banged against the cabin, the roof, the well, even the dead horses. When it was over, she checked her face. It was bleeding, but not much. Her headache from the previous night had felt much worse, but her thirst intensified.

"Sawyer!" Cale shouted. "Get Miss Scott out of here! Ride out, catch up with Dillon and the boys. Maybe they've heard the gunfire and are coming back!"

"What about you?"

"Leave me here. I'm safe for now."

Hannah yelled: "No! We won't leave you!"

"Do it!" Cale shouted. Slowly he opened the door. "I'll cover you as best as I can, Miss Scott. When I start shooting, you run to Sawyer. Sawyer! You cover her too. Then y'all ride like blazes."

She started to protest again, but Cale opened up with his rifle, firing steadily despite having the use of only one arm. Irwin also began shooting. "Now! Run!" Cale shouted, and Hannah stood and raced toward the shack. A bullet clipped her collar. Another shot dug into the adobe wall as she ran, and a third struck the rocks at her feet and sent her sprawling against the side of the house. She thought she might cry as a bullet slammed into the adobe wall and sprayed her face with dust and dirt, blinding her. Next she felt someone's hands on her shoulders, and she half-crawled and was half-pulled to the safety of the far wall.

"She all right?" Cale asked. Two more bullets struck the roof of the shack.

Hannah blinked until she could see and nodded. Irwin answered Cale and helped Hannah to her horse. She pulled her hat tightly on her head as her feet found the stirrups. Irwin swung into his saddle, reloaded his rifle, then lashed out at Hannah's horse and spurred his own mount. The two galloped out of the canyon as their assailant opened fire again. Hannah hung low against the horse, half-expecting to feel a bullet burn through her back, shattering bones and vital organs. At least, she guessed that was how it felt to be shot and killed. She could base her thoughts only on those silly half-dimers she read to Paco when he was sick.

But no bullet struck her, and the firing finally stopped. Still, she and Irwin rode hard until they had turned hard into an arroyo and rested their horses. Irwin shoved his rifle into the scabbard and handed Hannah his canteen, which she opened and drank greedily.

After handing the canteen to Irwin and letting him

drink, she took off her hat, wiped away the sweat mixed with tears, and then saw the three fresh holes in her hat. Two were in the wide brim and another was a gaping tear in the crown. Her heart pounded. She felt sick again. Then Irwin capped the canteen and said grimly, "We need to ride. Find the boys. Get help."

Hannah nodded, shoved on her ruined hat, and kicked her horse into a gallop, following Irwin, hating herself for leaving the wounded rancher behind.

She saw the rising dust after a few minutes, probably at the same time Irwin did, for both reined in their horses simultaneously and pointed ahead. A short while later, Dillon and Striker rounded a bed of boulders, slowed their lathered horses, and stopped in front of Hannah and Sawyer. The black cowboy pried a plug of tobacco from his cheek and tossed it to the ground.

"Where's the boss?" Dillon asked.

Irwin jerked his thumb back. "At Maggot's. We got waylaid by some guy in the rocks with a repeater. Mr. Cale made me get Hannah out of there, find y'all. Where's the other boys?"

"Back with them horses," Dillon said. "Let's get to Maggot's!"

Hannah turned her horse around. Sawyer protested, but she knew he couldn't argue for long—not with Julian Cale in trouble. The argument was cut even shorter when Striker pointed ahead. She looked up and saw the thick smoke blackening the sky. A groan escaped Hannah's lips as she remembered Sawyer splashing the inside and outside of Kibbee's shack with forty-rod whiskey and coal oil. She thought of

Cale inside that death trap, wounded, probably being burned alive.

The Concord pulled into the wagon yard at Fort Stockton at dusk. Pete waited until the trailing dust settled, wrapped the reins around the set brake, and dropped from the driver's boot. His knees bent forward, popping, and a sharp pain raced up his spine. Slowly he rose, feeling five times his age, and opened the stagecoach door, then stumbled and fell as the mutt leaped into his arms and licked his face.

Buddy Pecos pulled the cur off, using a small rope as a combination collar and leash. Pete stood, trying to ignore the catcalls from the station hands, and took control of the dog. It was part blue heeler, with some shepherd and collie, Pete guessed, along with other blood: wolf, perhaps; coyote; Comanche mongrel. He was friendly, though, and hungry despite having practically snorted up the two men's supply of jerky, hardtack, and stale biscuits.

''What you gonna do with that thing?'' Pecos asked.

''I figured to give him to the kids.''

Pecos snorted, shaking his head, and pulled out his cigarette papers and tobacco. Pete looked at the dog, who started scratching his left ear with his hind leg, whining. He had thought about naming the dog Apollo but decided the Greek gods might strike him dead for such an insult. The dog was ugly, not too smart, and really needed a bath.

''So,'' a feminine voice sounded behind him, ''is that a paying customer or simply freight?''

Pete turned. Jill Coffey's green eyes blinked coyly

and she stepped forward. She wore a tan riding outfit with a red blouse. Her dark hat hung on her back, secured with a latigo string of woven horsehair. Pecos struck a lucifer and lit his cigarette. The dog quit scratching and rolled over on its side.

"How are you?" Jill asked pleasantly, but her expression changed when she saw the bruises on Pete's face. "Oh, my goodness. What happened to you?"

"You know," Pete said.

She started to say something, a denial more than likely, but hesitated, then finally shrugged and smiled. "I told you I played to win," she said matter of factly.

"You didn't tell me you played that way."

Pete handed the rope to Pecos, who flicked away his unfinished cigarette, glanced at the dog, then Jill, and led the mutt to the stables. His contempt for the dog and gambler was equal. You could tell by the look in his good eye.

When Pecos was gone, Belissari told Coffey, "I guess you are a Black Widow after all."

Her eyes burned him now, and her voice was sharp. "You don't know—"

"I know enough. I know I live here. I have a reason, an interest in a stage line. It's just a game to you."

"It's more than a game, Pete!" Her face was bright red. She had lost her temper, which a gambler was never supposed to do. Pete was self-conscious that some of the stable hands were staring at them. He also thought Jill would break down and cry, but she found some measure of control and kept the tears in check as she raged.

"You think I'm that stupid character in those dreadful books. Well, I'm not. I don't write those, and I can't control what those hacks think up and sell. And let me tell you something else: I don't get a penny from those publishers. I make my living on the gambling circuit. That can be a halfway decent living when the cards are falling your way, but when you hit a losing streak, well, it's . . . it's . . . downright degrading.''

She caught her breath, then spit out more venom. ''And even when you're winning, it's not fun. A cowhand got caught cheating in one game at The Flat by Fort Griffin three years ago, and they shot him dead in front of me—so close that his blood splattered my face. Doc Holliday practically cut a fellow's head off with a knife in one game I was at. So I do what it takes, and I'd do anything to get out of this dollar-ante circuit for a chance to live like a lady—a real lady—and gamble with classy people in San Francisco.

''I won that stagecoach off your stupid partner and realized I was on to something. A stage line would bring a profit here. Even I could see that. I could sell out in a year, not have to worry about finding my next card game, and take my money and build a house in California. Maybe have a dream come true—for once. So, yes, Pete, I have my reasons for playing hard against you. It's not personal. I like you. I like you a lot. But I've been looking after myself for ten years, and this is my best chance.''

Their eyes met. Belissari tried to think of something to say, but his lips just moved silently. Jill Coffey brushed a strand of hair out of her eyes and looked at the stagecoach, shaking her head. ''I was going to ask you if you wanted supper,'' she said softly. ''The

Harvey House here is pretty good. But I'm not much hungry now. Good-bye, Pete.''

He sighed, his eyes following her as she stopped on a corner and reached into a purse, found a hanky, and dabbed her eyes. Then she turned left and disappeared. Belissari had lost his appetite too. At first he had been intrigued by Jill Coffey, followed by a slight crush, then anger. He didn't regret snapping at her, upsetting her. Instead, he felt something new, something deeper for the gambler: pity.

Chapter Eleven

Hannah pulled hard on the reins and almost slid to a stop. What was that the Reverend Cox would often say? "My heart jumped all the way to my throat!" That's how she felt when she saw the man riding toward her and the three cowboys. Then she recognized Julian Cale.

He slowly approached them, his long legs almost touching the ground, on the barebacked burro. The rancher had pulled off his left boot and wrapped a tourniquet above his ankle and some dirty rags, now completely stained with blood, around the bullet wound in his foot. She could see through Cale's smile and knew he must be in excruciating pain. Black soot crisscrossed his hauntingly pale face.

"You boys took your sweet time," he said in a raspy voice.

"We're sure glad to see you, boss," Dillon said, and Irwin mumbled something unintelligible.

"Yes sir," Striker echoed. "You get that fellow who ambushed you?"

Cale shook his head. "Shack caught fire." He nodded at his mount, which brayed. "Dumb beast here kicked over a lantern. I pulled myself up on this nag and somehow made it through the door. Nobody shot at me, so I'm guessing that whoever it was had already hightailed it out of there. Hadn't been gunfire for ten minutes, I guess.''

"Likely saw our dust,'' Dillon said.

Striker asked, "Want us to go after him?''

Men! Hannah said to herself, and swung from the saddle. Not one of them had asked his boss if he needed help, and that was obvious. They would sit on their mounts and talk about revenge and guns while Cale bled to death on that sorry-looking burro. She walked to her neighbor and offered her hand.

"Here, Mr. Cale,'' she said softly, "let me help you. We'll get you in the shade and I'll look at that bullet wound.''

Dillon grunted and spoke again. "That might not be such a good idea, ma'am. That assassin could be lurking about, then we'd all be in a fix.''

Hannah ignored him. Cale was right. If the gunman were still around, he would have shot Cale once he left the burning building. "Irwin, bring me your canteen,'' she said, "some whiskey if you have some. Come on, Mr. Cale. Let me help you.''

The rancher sighed. Groaning, he managed to get off the burro, caught his breath as he leaned against the animal, then took a tentative step toward Hannah. She gripped his hand, then looked horrified as the big man's eyes rolled back and he crashed against her.

The first time Pete Belissari saw Old Man Iverson's ranch, it had been a couple of dilapidated buildings that might have been comfortable to pack rats and coyotes. Then Hannah Scott bought the place and turned it into a home, though held together with spit and rawhide. Now, as he crested Wild Rose Pass and looked below, he had to rein his rented horse to a stop and survey the scene.

Smoke rose from the chimney in the cabin and cookshed, the children played baseball in the yard, and horses trotted or grazed in the two corrals. A cowboy, that dumb ox Irwin Sawyer more than likely, pounded horseshoes with a hammer in the new lean-to, the metallic clinks echoing across the countryside, and two other hands were hitching a team of grays to a buckboard parked by the covered patio. Across the road, Limpia Creek, full of snowmelt, flowed rapidly toward town ten miles away.

"Home's changed," he said, then laughed at himself. *Home.* He had been with Hannah less than a year and had never called this ranch home. At least his home. He thought about his argument with Jill Coffey, recalling his words: *"I live here. I have a reason. . . ."* In the past, his home had been wherever he threw his bedroll. In the mountains while chasing, catching, and breaking mustangs. In some rancher's bunkhouse while gentling other horses. In an Army stable, sometimes a hotel, or in his boyhood room at his parents' house in Corpus Christi. Maybe he was finally putting down roots.

"Come on," he said, and nudged the claybank toward the ranch, followed by that brainless hound he had finally named Obadiah to spite Pecos, whom he had left at Fort Stockton to guard the stagecoach. Obadiah was Buddy's real name.

"It's Pete!"

Belissari stepped away from his horse and let the children greet him with hugs, wet kisses on his cheeks, and a strong handshake from Chris. Obadiah wagged his tail.

"Where did you get the dog?" Paco asked.

"Oh, he just appeared on the road."

"What you gonna do with him?" Angelica said.

Pete shrugged. "I don't know. You know any kids who could give him a good home?"

The children charged him again—even sad, quiet Bruce—and knocked Pete to the ground. He clenched his teeth as they assaulted him with bear hugs that seemed to crush his sore ribs, not missing any of the bruises on his chest and arms. Then Obadiah joined the fray, and Cynthia squealed as the mutt licked her face.

"That's about as near as you'll ever get kissed," Paco said and laughed.

Cynthia stuck out her tongue at the little rogue and tripped him. Obadiah barked and jumped on Paco's chest. The boy let out an *oof!*, then broke out laughing as the other children piled on top of him. Somehow, the dog managed to escape the melee, and Pete used the opportunity to climb up and find his horse.

One of the cowhands in the yard was a jump ahead of him, though, and was leading the claybank to the corral. The other waddy smiled. Pete recognized Dillon, one of Julian Cale's top hands.

"That might be the ugliest critter I ever did see," Dillon said as the two men shook hands.

"He is not!" Angelica screamed. "He's adorable!"

"What's his name?" Paco asked.

"Obadiah."

"Come on," Chris said. "Let's see if he can fetch a baseball!" And the army of orphans and stupid dog raced across the yard to their make-do diamond. Pete sighed. He'd have to buy a new baseball soon. He had no doubt that Obadiah could fetch a ball, but he was equally sure that that mongrel would also eat it.

Pete brushed the dirt off his clothes and walked to the well to wash up. He was surprised that Hannah had not greeted him, and was curious why Cale's hired men were here.

"You look a mess," Dillon said.

Belissari nodded. "What brings you out here?" He soaked his bandanna in the oak bucket, then wiped his face and hands before tying the rag around his neck again.

"We had a run-in with some would-be horse thieves," Dillon said and nodded toward the Oldenburgs. "I'll let Miss Scott fill you in."

"Is Hannah all right?"

Dillon laughed. "That gal's tougher than an Apache. She's inside with Mr. Cale."

Pete met the two as he opened the door. Cale stood on crutches and hobbled outside, followed by Captain Jack Leslie as the Army doctor barked orders: "You stay off that leg for at least a week, Julian. You disobey my orders and I swear I'll saw that limb off. Dillon, you hear me? You make sure your boss stays in bed."

Cale glared at Belissari. "Seems like every time I help you out, I'm the one who gets shot to pieces." He turned back to Hannah and said softly, "I'm mighty grateful for your help and kindness, ma'am."

"Just get better, Mr. Cale."

Pete watched as the rancher slowly made his way to the buckboard, cursing Dillon and the other cowboy from top to bottom as they tried to help him. Dillon climbed onto the wagon seat after Cale, released the brake, and got ready to drive, but the rancher, still cursing, snatched the reins from the cowboy's hands and whipped the team furiously. His booming voice could still be heard long after the buckboard was out of sight.

Captain Leslie stuck a cigar in his mouth and pointed at the bruise underneath Pete's left eye. "Man or beast?" he asked.

Pete smiled. "Depends on your interpretation."

"Need my services?"

"Not yet."

"You will. If there's one good thing I can say about you, Pete, it's that you never fail to help my civilian practice. And, Army pay being what it is, I can always use the extra cash." He tipped his hat to Hannah and strode toward his horse in the corral.

"A dog?" Hannah asked after Leslie had gone. Pete and Hannah watched as the five children chased the animal around the barn and corrals, trying hopelessly to retrieve their baseball.

"It seemed like a good idea at the time."

Hannah laughed. "We have a lot to talk about. You hungry?"

"Starving."

The stretch from Cienega Creek to Shafter Station would be the most demanding. Well, none of the route seemed easy, but the road from Cienega to Shafter was awful, through a hard, unforgiving desert that would drain a horse's strength in no time. Once at Shafter Station, the team would be switched for Cash Hardee's strong Americans for the last, long leg, where Belissari wanted his fastest animals in case it came down to a horse race from Shafter to Presidio. But the key was Cienega Station. That's why Pete wanted the Oldenburgs there, and not here at Wild Rose Pass.

"Chris, I got a chore for you," Belissari said that evening as they rested on the porch. Obadiah's tail thumped against the side of the cabin as the teenager scratched his ears. The dog whined as Chris rose and walked over to the mustanger.

"Quiet!" Hannah scolded, and the dog, surprisingly, obeyed.

"Yes sir?" Chris said.

Pete explained his plan. "I need you and him"—he nodded at Irwin Sawyer, who was feeding the Oldenburgs in the corral—"to take those horses to Cienega Station and bring those Americans back here. And I want you back by Sunday at the latest. That's a hard ride. You think you're up to it?"

"Yes sir," he replied. "I'll try my best. But what if something happens? What if we can't make it back in time?"

"Hannah's going to see if she can borrow a team from Mr. Cale. But I really want that team from Cienega. They'd be prefect for the run to town."

"When should we leave?"

"First light."

After supper, Pete walked to the smaller, original corral to check on Poseidon, Duck Pegasus, and Lightning Flash, not to mention the horse he had rented at Fort Stockton. He wanted to make sure that oaf Sawyer wasn't starving them or fattening them, and to his surprise, he found the animals in prime condition. Then again, he hadn't been gone long.

He ran the race through his mind: Fort Stockton to Cleburne's post, to Stewart's ranch and Barrilla Springs. To Ezra Boone's spread, over Wild Rose Pass to Hannah's then on in to Fort Davis. From there to Marfa, to Perdiz Creek, to Cienega, to Shafter and on to Presidio.

One hundred eighty miles of rocks and cactus. Where anything could happen at any time.

He didn't like sending Chris and Sawyer away. Jill Coffey had tried to steal his horses; she might try something else. And although Belissari despised Irwin Sawyer, the cowhand came in handy a few times and would die to protect Hannah and those children. But it was worth the risk. He needed those Oldenburgs at Cienega Creek Station.

Sighing, he walked to his shed to turn in, but stopped when he saw the door was open. Silently he drew the .45 Colt from his holster, thumbed back the hammer as quietly as he could, and cautiously approached. *I'm getting paranoid,* he thought. But he'd play it safe. With the gun barrel, he pushed open the door wider and stared inside at the blackness.

"Come on out of there!" he said.

Silence.

"I know you're in there, so come on out!"

A horse whinnied from the corral.

With his left hand, Belissari found a match in his shirt pocket and struck it against the door frame. He saw the movement in his bed immediately, shook out the match, and crouched against the outside wall, stifling a yell.

"Come on out!" Pete yelled. "Or I'll shoot!"

He heard the noise then, and trying to scramble to his feet, slipped and fell forward, the revolver heavy in his outstretched arm. Belissari looked up at the doorway as Obadiah stared at him, yawned, and licked his face.

Chapter Twelve

Sheriff Tyler ''Slick'' Slaughter read over the rules one more time in front of a crowd at Gallager's Saloon. Since Fort Stockton was the county seat of Pecos County, Slaughter had no jurisdiction here, but he said he was serving as a ''friend of the post office and of fair play.''

Buddy Pecos snorted at that remark.

The town was like Fort Davis in that both were county seats and served nearby Army posts, but the similarities ended there. Here the mountains were miles away, and the wind stirred up alkali dust that settled on tack, clothes, even food. Originally called Saint Gall, Fort Stockton had served as county seat since Pecos County was organized ten years ago. It had grown from a campsite on the Old San Antonio Road to a military post's parasite community to solid commercial center of adobe and stone. Fort Stockton wasn't as pretty as its nearest neighbor, but it definitely was serviceable. Also unlike Fort Davis, the town of Fort Stockton prospered from hard-working farmers who were served by an honest German-Irish sheriff.

Unfortunately, most of the race would be contested where Slick Slaughter was the law.

Slaughter pulled a pocket watch from his vest

pocket and snapped it open. Smiling, he announced: "My watch has been set by the clock at the Bank of Presidio. Judges will be stationed at Fort Davis, Captain Jack Leslie of the United States Tenth Cavalry; Marfa, Father Ignacio Esperanza; Shafter, 'Alabama Bob' Bryan of the Presidio Mining Company; and Presidio, the honorable Judge William Paul McGrath.

"My watch says that it is eight thirty-nine. At nine o'clock sharp, the race will begin. First, we'll draw to see who runs today, and who leaves tomorrow. Gentlemen and lady"—he bowed at Jill Coffey—"would you like to cut cards for the honor?"

"Not against her," Buddy Pecos said, and the crowd laughed heartily, though Pete knew his friend wasn't joking.

"A coin flip, then?" Slaughter asked, still smiling.

Pecos and Coffey nodded. Slaughter slid the watch into his pocket and found a silver dollar. "I'll toss this in the air. Miss Coffey, since we're all Texas gentlemen, you'll do us the honor of calling heads or tails before it hits the ground." Jill nodded, Slaughter flipped the piece of silver high over his head, and the gambler said evenly, "Heads."

It's probably a two-headed coin, Belissari thought and watched as the dollar dropped at Slaughter's feet.

"Tails!" Slaughter shouted.

Groans and cheers mixed through the crowd, and Pete watched several soldiers, farmers, and town merchants exchange money. They had been betting on the coin flip. This race must be the biggest thing to happen in Fort Stockton since . . . since . . .

Slaughter interrupted his thoughts. "Mr. Pecos," he said, "you get to go first."

''Well,'' Pecos said, ''since we're all Texas gentlemen here, I'll run tomorrow. Miss Coffey can go first.''

The crowd cheered. Slaughter and Coffey frowned. Pete smiled. Second was the place to run. They'd have an advantage at the end, knowing what time they had to beat.

''Well—'' Slaughter began, but the town mayor cut him off.

''It is his choice,'' the big man said in a hard German accent. ''He won the coin flip. He can go second if he likes.''

Slaughter regained his composure, picked up his dollar, and nodded. ''Very well. Miss Coffey, I suggest you get your men and stagecoach ready. And may the better team win!''

''No word yet,'' Pete said after climbing aboard the Concord beside Pecos. Belissari pulled up the collar of his mackinaw and blew into his cupped hands to fight the morning chill.

''How you figure it?'' Pecos asked, releasing the brake and easing the stagecoach out of the wagon yard and toward Gallager's Saloon.

Pete shrugged. ''Maybe they haven't arrived at Presidio yet. Twenty-four hours doesn't allow for many setbacks. Road could be out. Could have lost a wheel.''

''Wire could be down,'' Pecos suggested.

Belissari's head bobbed in silent agreement.

''They could have cut the telegraph wire,'' Buddy continued, ''to keep us in the dark so we don't know what time we have to beat.''

"We'll know something by the time we reach Fort Davis or Marfa," Pete said. "You ready?"

It was Buddy's turn to shrug. He halted the stage in front of the saloon where another crowd had gathered to see the second stagecoach off. The turnout was smaller, Pete noticed, than yesterday, probably because the newness of the event was gone, or the fact that Fort Stockton was a working town so the men and women didn't have two mornings to waste, or, maybe, because the people here liked Jill Coffey better than Pecos and Belissari.

Whatever. This time the mayor explained the rules because Slick Slaughter had escorted Jill Coffey back to Fort Davis yesterday afternoon. A Pecos County deputy sheriff drew a pocket revolver from his coat and fired a round into the air when the mayor, watching his watch closely, called out, "Go!"

The Concord sped out of town, bouncing uncomfortably until Pecos settled the team into a fast gait. The old Confederate sharpshooter glanced at Belissari's feet and smiled. "What happened to them boots Hannah got you?" he shouted above the wind and clattering hooves.

"Moccasins are lighter," Pete said. "Didn't want us to carry any unnecessary weight."

It was eleven o'clock when the stage pulled into Dusty Cleburne's trading post. At least, Pete thought that was the time from the sun's position. Cleburne didn't own a clock or a watch, and he was still sleeping off a three-day drunk when Pete and Buddy arrived. The two men dropped from the Concord and washed down stale sourdough biscuits with bitter coffee while four Mexicans changed the team.

Then they were back in the driver's boot, screaming profanities at the fresh horses and raising thick dust across the broken country of creosote, cactus, and dust. A coyote studied the travelers curiously from a safe distance—the only life, other than a couple of roadrunners, that Pete and Buddy saw between the trading post and Captain W. J. Stewart's ranch.

Stewart was a bronzed man with a white beard of barbed wire and cottonwood trunks for arms. He had settled in this country back when the only travelers were Kwahadis on the Comanche War Trail. He greeted the stagecoach personally and helped two black cowboys change the horses as his Mexican wife served Pecos and Belissari tamales and coffee.

"How we doin', Capt'n, compared with Jill Coffey's coach?" Pecos asked as Stewart backed the new team toward the wagontongue.

Stewart glanced at the sky. Like Cleburne, he had no need for amenities such as watches and clocks. The sun, he often said, never needs winding. No one dared to ask him what he did on a cloudy day.

"Pert near the same, I reckon," he replied.

Minutes later, they were on the road again. Pecos handed Belissari the reins. "You take her a spell!" he ordered. "I'm gonna try to get some shut-eye. And don't stop for no dogs!" He pulled his battered hat over his eyes, crossed his arms, and bent his head until his chin rested on his chest. Then he bounced around like a greenhorn on a bronc.

The only man who could sleep on a stage, Belissari thought, was a corpse. He concentrated on the road, however, learning the feel of the reins in his fingers, studying each horse's tendencies, strengths, and weaknesses, much as he would a mustang he was breaking to be a saddle horse.

In a couple of hours, they'd be at Barrilla Springs. Pete wondered what kind of reception they'd get.

"How we doin'?" Pecos cried out as the stage slid to a dusty stop in front of the station.

Horace Griggs pulled a huge, open-faced watch from his brown pants and squinted. Luke Hopkins stepped out of the building, took a snort of whiskey, then tossed the pewter flask to Buddy Pecos as soon as the driver dropped to the ground. Belissari climbed down beside Pecos, who took a sip from the flask and offered it to Pete. Belissari declined.

" 'Bout five minutes ahead of 'em," Griggs said. "Both of y'all made pretty good time."

"This ain't the stretch I'm worried about," Pecos said, tossing the whiskey to Griggs. "Got any grub?"

In a normal run, Barrilla Springs would be the last stop for the jehu and messenger. Here, two other men would take over the stage and lead a fresh team to the next stops until reaching another home station where they, in turn, would be spelled. But this wasn't a normal run. They hadn't had time to hire other drivers and shotgun riders, and Pete and Buddy wouldn't have trusted anyone else to run this race, so they'd have to travel the entire journey alone.

Pecos was right too. From Fort Stockton to Barrilla Springs was the easy part of the route. It would be dark soon, and they'd have to pick their way through the Davis Mountains, up and down Wild Rose Pass to Hannah's place, to Fort Davis and Marfa and deep into the rugged terrain surrounding Shafter and through the wicked desert leading to Presidio.

Pecos and Belissari wolfed down Hopkins's fiery chili and bitter coffee, relaxed while Griggs greased the axles, then found their spots in the front boot, with Buddy driving and Pete riding shotgun again, both men squinting as they drove out of Barrilla Springs toward the bright, sinking sun.

It was dusk when they reached Ezra Boone's ranch in the Davis Mountains. As soon as the teams were changed, Belissari lit the lanterns on each side of the Concord. With a crescent moon hidden by clouds, the lanterns would be their only light as they traveled the mountain road.

Pecos slowed the pace a bit. ''Why don't you try and get some sleep, pard?'' Belissari snorted at the thought of sleeping in this bouncing contraption, but he realized how tired he was, so he laid the shotgun at his feet, pulled down his hat and, much to his surprise, was asleep in minutes.

Screaming profanity and a violent lurch jerked him awake. From the glow of the lanterns he saw Pecos, feet braced against the front boot, leaning as far back as he could, pulling the reins with all his might as the horses snorted and the Concord slid to the left. Pete grabbed the metal railing to hold on until the stagecoach slid to a stop and a bang as the left rear wheel went off the road and the Concord slammed to its axle, the wheel hanging over a ditch or an arroyo.

Pecos pulled back the brake and dropped to the ground. Pete started to do the same on his side, but when he peered over, he realized he'd be falling a good fifty feet. He swore and scrambled to the other side and leaped off the coach.

Buddy was behind him, looking at a fallen juniper in the middle of the road just after a curve. How Pecos had managed to get the stagecoach around that tree he'd never know. But that Pecos had managed to keep the Concord from going into the canyon he'd always be grateful for.

"Check the horses, Pete," Pecos ordered, and Belissari walked toward the front of the coach. The horses were lathered, winded, and frightened, but otherwise fine. Belissari went over their legs and hooves while Pecos peered under the coach.

"Axle ain't broke," Pecos said.

"Horses are all right," Pete said.

Belissari patted one of the horses' necks and watched Buddy head back down the road, strike a match, and study the fallen tree. He shook out the match after a minute. From the look on his friend's face, Pete knew that it wasn't wind or lighting that had knocked that tree into the road. "Ax," Pecos said, and punctuated his comment with an oath. Then he looked at the stuck stagecoach and studied the rear wheel.

"How's your back?" he asked. "Looks like we've got some liftin' to do."

Chapter Thirteen

They should be here by now, Hannah thought, watching the swinging pendulum on the Waterbury wall clock. It chimed on the hour as Christopher—no, he wanted to be called Chris now—and Irwin opened the door. Irwin found the blue enamel coffeepot and filled two mugs, one of which Chris picked up and sipped.

"Since when did you start drinking coffee, Chris?" Hannah asked, smiling.

The tall teen shrugged. He and Irwin had returned yesterday morning with the horses from Cienega Creek just as Pete wanted. Now they were waiting on the stage. Hannah looked at the clock again. The smile disappeared.

"You want me to go lookin' for 'em?" Irwin asked.

Hannah shook her head.

"They should have been here an hour ago."

"They'll be here."

Irwin blew his coffee, and Chris copied the cowboy. The clock ticked. From their beds, one of the children yawned. Outside, Obadiah whined and scratched the door. Hannah started to scold the dog, but she heard something else. She opened the door and stepped into the darkness, followed by Chris and Irwin.

Obadiah's tail thumped, an owl hooted, and the

wind rustled through the oaks and boulders. And then she heard it again, the jingle of braces, squeak of wheels, muffled hooves, and unmistakable profanity of Buddy Pecos.

A few minutes later the stagecoach bounded out of the darkness and into the yard, lit up by two lanterns hanging from the patio. Chris and Irwin were already moving to unhitch the team before Pete and Buddy slowly climbed from the front boot. Their clothes were dirty, eyes bloodshot, faces red from the wind and cold. She quickly realized she should bring them coffee and cold sandwiches, but the children, now wide awake, were one jump ahead of her.

Dressed only in their sleeping gowns, Cynthia brought the sandwiches and Angelica the coffee cups while silent Bruce struggled, carrying the hot coffeepot with both hands. Hannah started to help him but decided against it. Paco sliced the air with his wooden sword, screaming excitedly and showing off for Pete and Pecos before Chris snapped, "Shut up, Paco, before you spook the horses!"

Wearily Pete walked toward her. He looked terrible, but Hannah figured that half the time she saw him, he looked like he'd been trampled. He swallowed a hunk of sandwich and drank coffee. Behind him, Pecos was nodding politely at whatever Angelica was saying while barking an occasional order at Irwin and Chris, who harnessed the fresh team to the Concord.

"You're running late," Hannah said.

Pete nodded. "Ran off the road a ways back. A tree just happened to fall down just around a bend in the road."

Hannah clenched her fists and bit her lip. One day

she'd pull out all of Jill Coffey's beautiful hair, then feed it to her. They looked at each other for a minute. Pete started toward her but Pecos yelled, "Let's ride, pardner!" The Texan was already climbing back into the driver's boot.

Frowning, Pete took another sip of coffee, tossed the rest on the ground, and handed the empty cup to Hannah. Shoving the unfinished sandwich into his coat pocket, he sprinted to the stagecoach, climbed up beside Pecos, and with the crack of a whip and a shout from Buddy, the Concord pulled out of the light and into the darkness, Obadiah chasing and barking at the wagon for a good hundred yards.

Captain Jack Leslie puffed a cigar in front of Boskirk's livery as the stagecoach arrived at Fort Davis an hour later. Pecos had practically flown down the ten-mile stretch from Hannah's ranch to town.

"You guys are running behind," Leslie said.

Pete and Buddy stayed in the boot, partly to save time, mostly because they were too tired to move.

"What was Coffey's final time?" Belissari asked.

The Army doctor shrugged. "Wire's down between Shafter and Presidio. We haven't heard yet, but some of the gamblers at the Headquarters Saloon sent a galloper this afternoon to find out. You should know what you have to beat by the time you reach Marfa. But"—He looked at his watch—"you're an hour behind them now."

Pete nodded. The stable hand shouted, "All set!" The Concord surged forward and south toward Marfa. "Ride hard!" Leslie cried out behind them. "I got five bucks riding on y'all!"

* * *

They didn't learn anything specific in Marfa, mainly because the official judge was asleep. The desk clerk at the Marfa Hotel said he had heard the Coffey coach made the journey in twenty-two hours, but the town marshal thought it was twenty-one and change. A whiskey drummer said they were an hour, maybe two, behind the Coffey coach's time, but a cowboy said, no, they were a good three or four hours behind and might as well call it quits and buy him a drink, and a hurdy-gurdy girl from the dance hall by the railroad tracks said she thought they were about dead even. So the marshal decided he'd go find out for sure and wake up the good padre Esperanza, but by then the Concord was bouncing down Main Street, crossing the railroad tracks, and speeding toward the next stop at Perdiz Creek.

"Twenty-one hours and seventeen minutes," the station master at Perdiz Creek said. "That's the time you have to beat." The silver-haired gent stifled a yawn and tossed some cooked beef to Pecos. He looked inside his adobe shack for a few seconds—at a clock, Belissari guessed—yawned again, and added, "You're about a half-hour behind their time here."

Buddy Pecos nodded, chewed on the thought and food, and handed the beef to Belissari. Pete took a bite and spit it out. It was rancid. He gagged and reached for the canteen in the boot as Pecos whipped the reins and forced the stagecoach back onto the dark, bumpy road.

Pecos drove the fresh team furiously, refusing to slow down even after the stagecoach leaned on two wheels around a curve before righting itself. Pete thought his stagecoach nausea might return, so he gripped the seat. The spell passed, however, and he stared through the yellow light at the straining horses and endless road in front of him.

They made it to the next stop in a couple of hours. Cienega Station was an adobe hut and stone corral that Milton Faver rented to a couple of Mexican sheep-herders. Faver owned the best, if not the most, country in these parts. The handful of acres at Cienega Creek was probably Faver's worst investment, but it looked priceless to Pete Belissari.

From the dim light of lanterns and campfire, Pete saw those beautiful Oldenburgs in the corral, ready to be hitched to the Concord. He reached down to take a cup of coffee and some tortillas from a Mexican girl while the horses were changed. He barely tasted either food or coffee.

"These horses as good as you say they are?" Pecos asked before biting off a giant wad of tobacco and working it into his left cheek.

Belissari tossed the empty cup to the pretty Mexican girl. "*Gracias.*" To Pecos: "They're the best we got."

"They better be." Pecos released the brake and cracked the whip.

Past Cienega Creek, the rode began to slice through the rugged Chinati Mountain range. The German horses, however, showed no sign of weariness. In fact, they barely slowed down. *We've got a chance,* Pete thought. The Oldenburgs could get them to Shafter, then Cash Hardee's fast Americans could sprint the rest of the way to Presidio.

The Concord crested a hill and began descending into Shafter. Pete could see the lights of town below and the graying sky in the east, though full dawn was a few hours away. And he could make out something else: a brighter light, rippling in the distance, just south of town.

Pecos barely slowed as the stage raced past the WELCOME TO SHAFTER sign. Men were filing out of The Men's Clubhouse and all-night saloons, pointing at the orange light that Pete now knew must be a fire. Other men were running along, some of them armed with rifles and shotguns, gesturing excitedly.

Belissari glanced at Pecos, but his friend concentrated on the road as they traveled down Main Street and splashed across Cibolo Creek. Pete kicked the stagecoach and swore. He knew what was burning long before the Concord pulled in front of Shafter Station.

"What happened?"

Belissari dropped from the boot and fought his way through the crowd at Goldman's and McBride's station. Flames engulfed the roof and inside of the adobe shack. A few men were working a bucket brigade from the cistern to the house, but it was hopeless. Pete looked at the big corral, saw where the rails had been knocked down. Cash Hardee's hard-running Americans were gone.

"Goldman!" he shouted. "McBride!"

"Pete!"

Belissari turned. Dave Goldman shoved past two bearded miners. The stationmaster's face was covered in soot and blood.

"It was Apaches!" someone shouted, though there hadn't been Indian trouble in years.

"Run off their stock," another one commented, "shot that poor Mexican boy."

"Somebody better get the Army down here!"

Goldman gripped Pete's shoulders with his left hand. His right held an empty revolver. Goldman's eyes were glassy, his voice breathless. "They just hit us. Got the horses! Shot poor Felipe in the shoulder, but I think he'll be all right."

Felipe was the stable hand they had hired. "Where's McBride?"

The stationmaster took a deep breath. "Happy took a bullet in his thigh. They're patching him and Felipe up. Pete, I'm sorry, man. Last thing I expected was Apaches!"

"This look like an Apache to you?" Both men turned as a big miner with a beard as dark as night shoved a small man in buckskins forward. The man's wrists were bound behind his back, his left shoulder stained crimson and seeping blood from a bullet hole. "I shot this bushwhacker off his horse," the miner said. "He was ridin' with them horse thieves, I'll swear to it. Seen it with my own eyes. Apache!" He snorted.

The prisoner had long, dark hair, and his face was painted with vermilion. He wore greasy leather and moccasins, and even had a red silk scarf tied over his head, but he was Mexican, not Apache. Pete recognized him as one of Cash Hardee's riders. So *Un Mal Hombre* had thrown in with Jill Coffey.

"Let's string him up!" someone yelled, and like a Sunday choir, other voices joined in.

Buddy Pecos stepped into the center of the circle. Talk stopped. All eyes fell upon the towering, one-eyed gunman. "Patch him up," Pecos ordered. "Then take him to Fort Davis and lock him up. In the Army stockade, not Sheriff Slaughter's jail. Tell Capt'n Leslie I said so."

Buddy's pale eye stared at the wounded prisoner. "We'll sort this thing out later, *amigo.* And we hang horse thieves." He looked at Pete. "Let's ride."

"But you need fresh horses for that final run," Goldman said.

"We'll have to make do," Pecos said.

It was light now, and the Oldenburgs were tiring but still game. Pete saw the rider galloping toward them. He pulled the Parker shotgun from the boot, thumbing back both hammers. The horse, a bay, slid to a stop and spun around, and the rider began loping south along the road, waiting for the stagecoach to catch up. He knew what he was doing, Pete thought, and was a pretty good horseman.

The man wore the light blue pants, dark blouse, and tan hat of the United States Cavalry. He was black, with a long, dark beard, probably one of the buffalo soldiers from Fort Davis. When the stagecoach paralleled him, he shouted, "Mr. Pecos, Mr. Everhart sent me! Road's washed out just north of town! We gots to take another road!"

Pecos sprayed the side of the wagon with tobacco juice and nodded. "Lead the way, soldier. And much obliged!"

"There's a fork just a mile down the road!" the

trooper said. "Follow me!" Spurring his bay, the man galloped in front of the coach.

Pete said nothing, but slowly he eased the hammers down on the shotgun and returned the weapon to the boot. He saw the fork in the road, saw the trooper turn to the right and gallop on, saw the soldier rein in hard and wave his arms frantically as Buddy Pecos took the left road and never slowed down.

"Never trusted a bluebelly!" Pecos said.

I hope you're right, Belissari said to himself.

The road was hard, but serviceable—definitely not washed out. Pete's throat was dry. When the leaders began to falter, he pulled the shotgun up and fired a barrel into the air. The horses picked up speed, and Pete pulled the second trigger. Pecos's whip cracked like another gunshot as the Concord bounced and rolled into Presidio, through the residential area, sending chickens, dogs, and a drunk running for cover before entering the business district.

Buddy pulled hard on the reins and the stage slowed and stopped in front of the Bank of Presidio. Slick Slaughter stood on the boardwalk in front of the adobe and stone building beside Dean Everhart, Jill Coffey, the gunman Tubac, Judge William Paul McGrath, and two other businessmen. "Time!" yelled the judge, looking at his gold watch, and disappeared in a thick cloud of white dust.

Chapter Fourteen

"Twenty-one hours," Judge McGrath said, "and . . . seventeen minutes." He looked up skeptically, stepped inside the bank to check his timepiece against the regulator clock there, and finally reappeared, tugging on his red mustache and smiling.

"Twenty-one, seventeen," he repeated. He swore softly, quickly apologized to Jill Coffey, shook his head, and commented, "Reckon we needed a seconds hand."

Unbelievable! A tie!

They had traveled one hundred and eighty miles in just more than twenty-one hours. And for what? Nothing. They would report the raid and shootings at Shafter Station to Slaughter, complain about the suspicious fallen juniper in the middle of the road and the soldier's ruse just outside of town. But they couldn't prove anything—unless the wounded Mexican talked, and even then Coffey and Hardee would deny his allegations.

Jill Coffey smiled at Pete, but the tired mustanger didn't return it.

"Well," Judge McGrath said. "We'll have to discuss this with the postmaster. Miss Coffey, Mr. Everhart, let's say we meet at Paloma's Café at noon. I can say one thing: No matter who wins the mail contract, if y'all can make that run consistently in twenty-one hours, there will be a lot of happy folks in this part of Texas.''

''Except the passengers,'' Pete whispered, and with a grimace and groan, he climbed off the stagecoach.

Pete Belissari christened Dean Everhart's Concord the *Argo,* after the fifty-oared ship made of Mount Pelion pines that Argus built for Jason in Greek mythology. Buddy Pecos called it something else, and back in January, Pete would have agreed with him.

Yet Pete had to accept the fact that the *Argo*—with help from Julian Cale's Oldenburgs—had saved Hannah, Everhart, Pecos, and himself from losing the race. Now they had another chance, and Pete was confident they would win.

Jill Coffey's team had made the run without any problems. Pete and Buddy had endured a near catastrophic wreck and lost time in the Davis Mountains, and one team of horses had been forced to run an extra twenty miles without rest.

He wasn't taking any chances, though. They had rented a crumbling jacal and corral spitting distance from the Rio Grande. The *Argo* was in the corral along with the horses, and Buddy Pecos was patrolling the perimeter with the double-barreled Parker.

The postmaster, Coffey, Everhart, and county officials had agreed on a second race to determine the mail contract. This race would run from Presidio to Fort Stockton—and this one would carry passengers, three each. The coaches would also be running simultaneously, another change from the first running. The race was scheduled for Wednesday. Four days from now.

Belissari sat inside the rundown adobe shack at a rough-hewn table across from a Ranger sergeant. The lawman pulled his blond goatee and listened patiently as Pete spewed out his charges against Coffey, Hardee, and Slaughter. Belissari filed a complaint on the Shafter shootings with Slaughter—he knew that would be fruitless, but the man was the county sheriff—then voiced his allegations to Judge McGrath and the Presidio marshal before turning to the Texas Rangers, who were equally uninterested in the schemes against the new stagecoach line.

"Mr. Belissari," the Ranger said, "I understand, but there's just nothing the Rangers can do right now. Or the county sheriff, or the marshal, or even the Pinkertons for that matter. There's just not enough evidence."

Buddy Pecos walked inside without his shotgun. That meant Dean Everhart had spelled him. The lanky gunman found a seat by the window and began rolling a cigarette.

"They stole our horses at Shafter Station," Pete argued.

"All of which were recovered a few miles up Cibolo Creek," the Ranger responded.

"They shot a fourteen-year-old boy and a blind man!"

"I know. I'm sorry. You've got one of those men locked up at Fort Davis. If he talks, maybe you can file charges against Coffey or Cash Hardee. Believe me, I'd like to see *Un Mal Hombre* swing, and I don't like that gambler or the two-bit assassin she employs.

And I voted for Mr. Pecos, not Tyler Slaughter.'' The Ranger rose and placed a wide-brimmed hat on his head.

''I wish you men luck,'' he said, ''and I wish there was something we could do.'' He cleared his throat. ''My unofficial advice to you is to use Texas justice.''

''What's that?''

''If the law doesn't work, do it yourself,'' the man said, and left.

Pete was silent for a few minutes. Pecos crushed out his cigarette, walked to the corner of the hut, and dropped heavily onto the rickety bed. He looked pale.

''You all right?'' Belissari asked.

''Tuckered out.''

''Me too.''

Belissari dosed in the chair for a few minutes, jumping awake and reaching for his holstered Colt. Someone was knocking at the door. He glanced at Pecos, still snoring loudly in the bed, slowly rose, and walked forward, thumbing back the hammer on his revolver before jerking open the door and staring outside.

''What are you doing here?'' he asked.

Hannah didn't really know why she came to Presidio. Maybe it was to be with Pete. Maybe it had to do with the fact that she was a partner in the stagecoach operation. Probably it was because she just couldn't sit and wait at home for word on what was going on. So she left Irwin and Chris at the ranch, along with a couple of cowboys Julian Cale had sent over, and took the buckboard south with Paco, Angelica, Cynthia, and Bruce. And Obadiah too. That stupid mutt wouldn't stop following them, and by the time she realized she should have tied the dog up, it was too late.

Now the children played with the dog in the yard while Dean Everhart was perched on the *Argo* with a shotgun. Buddy Pecos slept in the worst-looking bed Hannah had ever seen, and she and Pete sipped coffee boiled in the silty, foul-tasting water from the Rio Grande. The rented jacal wasn't fit for a worm. The crackers they were eating were stale, and Pete had to cut away the mold on the cheese with his pocketknife.

Yet Hannah didn't regret coming.

''Whoever cut the telegraph wire knew what he was doing,'' Pete was explaining. ''He spliced the line with a rubber band. Took the workers almost two days to find it and repair it. Anyway, I got a wire from Doc Leslie. He says Slick Slaughter had his deputy raise a stink about keeping that bandit in the fort's stockade, as it wasn't Army business, made them transfer the prisoner to the county jail.''

''So he can conveniently escape,'' Hannah said.

''We'll see.''

''What about the trooper who tried to get you to take the wrong road?''

Pete shrugged. ''Buddy's guess is that he's either a deserter or had been drummed out.''

She remembered the court-martialed soldier who had shown up at the ranch with the gunman Tubac after Everhart lost the stagecoach to Jill Coffey in a card game. She described the man to Pete.

''That's him,'' Pete said. ''Not that it matters. There's no crime in trying to trick a couple of featherheads on a stagecoach to win a bet—or mail contract.''

He drank some coffee, forced it down, and continued: "Anyway, I'm going to take the Oldenburgs to Shafter Station tomorrow, bring the Americans back here for the first run."

"You're pretty confident we can win."

"We can. We'll be running right alongside the Coffey coach, so I don't expect any trees in the middle of the road. The catchy part will be at the stations we share with Jill: Marfa, Barrilla Springs, and those, where we'll both be changing teams. . . ."

"Must you call her *Jill*?" Hannah said.

"Sorry. Anyway, at those stops, it's important we arrive first. I'm not sure they'll be able to change teams simultaneously, so it's first come, first served." He smiled. "I'm prattling on like Paco." He took her hand in his. "I'm glad you're here."

None of the children had ever been to Mexico, so Hannah and Pete took them on the ferry across the river, found a place to eat in the small village and dined on tortillas, rice, beans, and spicy enchiladas. Naturally, Cynthia and Angelica didn't like the enchiladas, Bruce just picked at his food and Paco spit out the milk when he found out it came from a goat. But they loved the sopaipillas, drowning the pastry in honey, much to the delight of the woman who served as the café's cook, waitress, and owner.

They recrossed the river at sunset, then stopped on the way back to the rented house to watch a family of javelinas feed along the riverbank. It was dark when they turned down the dusty road toward the jacal and heard the gunshot.

"Stay here!" Pete shouted, drew his revolver, and

sprinted toward the house. Hannah waited only a couple of seconds before she told the children: "Stay! Don't move until we come for you!" And she took off after Pete.

Flames shot up behind the house, and Obadiah barked furiously, stretching the hemp reata that secured him to the jacal's porch. The Oldenburgs screamed, stampeding around the corral, pressing against the wood rails in an attempt to get away from the searing flames. It was only then that Hannah realized what was burning.

The *Argo*!

Two silhouetted figures appeared in front of the burning stagecoach, dragging another figure toward her. Hannah stepped forward, but the heat forced her back. She held her breath. Pete and Buddy Pecos carried an unconscious Dean Everhart to the center of the yard. The dog continued barking as volunteer firemen in their bib-front shirts drove a pump wagon into the yard, yelling excitedly, shouting orders. But Hannah knew it was hopeless. She could smell the coal oil someone has splashed on the *Argo* and knew it was far too late to save the Concord.

She looked at Everhart and grimaced. "Pete," she said, "he's hurt bad. He needs a doctor."

Judge McGrath frowned under his red mustache. "I don't like this one bit. No sir. Not one bit."

They sat in the hotel lobby after leaving the children asleep in the jacal and Everhart with the nearest thing Presidio had to a doctor, an Irish barber on the west side of town who patched up people and pulled teeth on the side. Two of the firemen had agreed to watch the children, Oldenburgs, and charred ruins of the Concord until Hannah, Pete, and Pecos returned.

"I ain't happy either," Buddy said, his bloodless face darkened by soot and Everhart's blood.

Pecos had been sleeping in the shack when Obadiah's barks awakened him. He rushed outside, saw the stagecoach already burning and fired a shot, missing, as two men fled into the darkness. Buddy raced to fight the blaze but almost tripped over Everhart, lying unconscious in the corral after being hit savagely from behind. Neither man could positively identify the raiders.

"How is Mr. Everhart?" McGrath asked.

Pete answered: "Broken collarbone, sprained wrist, and some cracked ribs. Concussion. Needed fifteen stitches. They pistol-whipped him pretty good."

"Well, we'll find out who burned your stagecoach and injured your partner. I won't tolerate this in my district. I suspect it was someone who had money on Coffey and Co."

"It *was* Jill Coffey," Hannah said, barely controlling her rage. "At least, she had it done."

McGrath cleared his throat. "Ma'am, you have no proof."

They were silent for a few minutes. The clock in the lobby chimed midnight. Sheriff Tyler Slaughter was nowhere to be found, and Jill Coffey had retired for the night. The town marshal, sitting beside the judge, looked equally uncomfortable. Buddy Pecos looked half-dead. Pete smoothed his mustache, and Hannah noticed some new gray hairs. Belissari wasn't even thirty years old.

‘‘What about getting the race pushed back until we get another stagecoach?’’ Pete asked.

Frowning, McGrath shook his head. ‘‘I’m afraid that can’t be done, sir. It just wouldn’t be proper and fair to Miss Coffey. No, I regret to say that unless you can come up with another stagecoach by Wednesday, you will have to forfeit the race to Coffey and Co. I’m sorry.’’

He rose quickly, in a hurry to be gone, and went upstairs to his room. The town marshal, a fat, bald man in a worn-out suit, stood up, tipped his hat, and walked out the door without speaking.

Hannah looked at Buddy Pecos, then her eyes met Pete’s. She sighed, defeated. ‘‘There isn’t another stagecoach within two hundred miles of here,’’ she said.

Pete stared absently out the hotel window. ‘‘Actually,’’ he said after a moment. ‘‘There is.’’

Chapter Fifteen

El fortín, as the Mexicans called Fort Leaton, was as impressive and intimidating as Hannah had been led to believe. Shortly after arriving in West Texas, she had heard the grim tales of murder within these adobe walls. Cash Hardee, folks said, once decapitated a thief and left the man's head on a fence post outside the compound as a warning.

Hannah and Pete rode through the massive gate just after dawn Sunday. A rooster crowed, two sentries watched carefully from the roof, and an elderly Mexican woman, her face almost burned black by the sun, collected eggs, followed by the ugliest and smelliest goat Hannah had ever seen. Belissari nodded toward the blacksmith's shop near the corral, and Hannah saw the stagecoach, a rotting wreck on four wheels.

"*That?*" Hannah asked.

"That," Pete replied.

She heard a door open and turned in her saddle to see a white-haired, goateed Mexican and two young boys approach them. The old man said something in Spanish to the youths. Pete nodded at Hannah, and they dismounted, handing the reins to the Mexicans.

"*Buenos días, Señor* Belissari," the man said as the horses were led away. He bowed at Hannah and added, "*Señorita.*"

"Tadeo," Pete said, "this is Hannah Scott. We would like to discuss buying the stagecoach with *Señor* Hardee." Pete had spoken in Spanish, but Hannah understood most of what he said. Tadeo's long, bony fingers ran through his flowing goatee. Finally, he nodded and opened the wooden door, motioning for them to follow.

"Are those . . . scalps?" She choked out the words, looking in disbelief at the cured strips of black hair hanging from a ceremonial lance on the wall in Hardee's dark office.

"Yeah," Pete replied. He looked nervous, his face pale, right hand resting on the butt of his holstered revolver. Belissari had not wanted Hannah to come to Fort Leaton, but she wouldn't listen. She was a partner in this stagecoach business and had argued that Hardee might be influenced by a woman. Pete responded by telling her about Hardee's Mimbres Apache wife. As she stared at the horrible "trophies," Hannah wondered which scalp belonged to Hardee's unfortunate bride.

In the end, Hannah won the argument as she usually did. This was her plan, though she had stolen it from the half-dime novel *Wild Times in Wichita* she had read to Paco. It would take two people, and they would need Buddy Pecos's help if it didn't work. They had left the sharpshooter and his buffalo rifle on the floodplain near the fort with these vague orders: "If we're not back by tonight, think of something and get us out of there."

Cash Hardee opened the door. He wore navy wool trousers tucked in black riding boots, a white shirt with pleated front, ivory buttons and stand-up paper collar, gold ring, black silk cravat, and a green waistcoat that had gone out of fashion in Sam Houston's day. He looked dressed for Sunday Mass, Hannah thought, except for the knife handle sticking out of his right boot top and the two shiny revolvers tucked in his waist.

His hair was close-cropped, and a brown and gray mustache covered a thin upper lip. He was tall, lean, and tan, with pale blue eyes and a mean scar traversing his forehead. After filling a tumbler with whiskey and downing it, Hardee smiled and said, "Well, well, well, if it isn't my favorite horse trader in all of Texas."

He spoke to Belissari, but his unnerving eyes never left Hannah.

"Seems like one of your vaqueros and some other bandits tried to steal our horses at Shafter Station," Pete said calmly. "Shot two of our men in the process."

Hardee clucked his tongue. "Can't get good help anymore. I'll fire the man if y'all don't hang him."

Belissari smiled, though Hannah knew it was a facade. Her own stomach was turning over, heart pounding, throat dry, and she knew Pete was just as uneasy. "Our stagecoach burned last night," Pete continued. "You wouldn't know anything about that, would you?"

"I was here all night," he said, still looking at Hannah.

"I figured that." Pete took a deep breath, exhaled, and continued. "But that's not why we're here. We're interested in taking that old stagecoach off your hands."

Hardee laughed, pulling a cigar from his waistcoat.

He bit off an end and spit it into a brass cuspidor, struck a match, and fired up the pungent tobacco.

"Belissari," Hardee said, "why would I sell you a stagecoach when I have a five-hundred-dollar bet riding on Coffey and Co. winning that mail contract?"

Now Pete chuckled. "Because," he said, "you're greedy, and you don't really think we can win with that old thing."

Hardee finally looked away from Hannah. She felt herself breathe again. The old scalphunter studied Belissari for a minute, puffed on his cigar, and after a while nodded. "All right, *amigo,*" he said. "But you know my rules. Poker, then business. First, however, we eat. I trust y'all haven't had breakfast yet. *Tadeo*!"

Hannah Scott had learned how to play poker in the Travis County orphanage, though she had never played for money before. Hardee had been genuinely impressed when she asked to sit in and even more pleased when Belissari folded his hand and quit the game. Now it was just two-handed poker, with Belissari leaning against the dark wall, smoking a cigarette. *That's how bad it is,* Hannah thought. *He's smoking.* The room was sparse: table, a few chairs, spittoon, dinner bell, and armoire. Tadeo, the Mexican servant, was gone. It was just Pete, Hannah, and Cash Hardee.

She looked her cards over. Hardee had dealt her a full house, jacks over tens. *This is it,* she thought. She bet five dollars. Hardee nodded, saw the bet, and raised five hundred. Belissari coughed and crushed out his cigarette. Hannah tossed more greenbacks into the pot.

"How many?" Hardee asked.

"I'm pat," she replied.

Nodding, Hardee said, "Dealer takes three." He tossed three cards onto the table and reached for the deck, but Hannah leaned forward and took his left hand in hers, turning it over, palm down, ogling his ring.

The band was gold with the Masonic emblem engraved on the front square, inlaid with twelve small diamonds. Hannah seriously doubted that Cash Hardee was a Mason. He probably stole the ring off a man he had killed.

"That's beautiful," she said, admiring the ring a few seconds more before looking up at the scalphunter. Hardee smiled. Hannah stroked his hand, turned it over, and quickly pulled out the three cards he had hidden up his sleeve.

"And what have we here?"

Cash Hardee swore violently and lunged out of his chair, but Belissari stepped forward, drew his Colt, and pressed the barrel against Hardee's temple, cocking the .45 with three intimidating clicks.

The scalphunter slipped back in his chair, his sinister eyes burning with hatred, face locked in a gruesome scowl. "I'll kill you for this, Belissari," he said. "Both of you."

Hannah pulled a piece of paper from her purse and slid it across the table. "This is a bill of sale for that stagecoach," she said. "I think two hundred dollars is more than a fair price. It also calls for the rental of two mules to pull the stage to Presidio. You can pick up the stock at the town livery. Sign it." She tossed him her brand-new Fairchild's fountain pen.

"This won't hold up in court," Hardee said, barely controlling his rage.

She smiled, recalling the advice Pete said a Texas Ranger had given him. *If the law doesn't work, do it yourself.* Hardee signed the document, which Hannah returned to her purse along with the pen. Then Cash Hardee laughed.

"All right, folks. Now, how do you two plan on getting out of here alive?"

Belissari nodded at Hannah, who stood up and rang the dinner bell. A minute later, Tadeo entered the room, his face expressionless.

"Tadeo," Belissari said in Spanish, "we have caught your boss cheating at cards. Now we need your help."

Hardee barked, "Tadeo, you cross me and I'll skin you alive!" Pete pressed his gun barrel harder against the killer's head.

"What of me do you wish?" Tadeo asked, and slowly he smiled.

Pete Belissari handed Tadeo a leather pouch when they reached the ferry at Presidio. The old servant had brought his wife, son, daughter-in-law, and two grandsons with him. They had left Cash Hardee bound and gagged in his armoire, where Tadeo assured Pete and Hannah that it would be hours, maybe even a day, before anyone looked for him. Then, with the Mexican's assurances to the guards that all was well, they left Fort Leaton with their horses, decaying Concord stagecoach and—most importantly—their scalps.

"No, *señor,*" Tadeo said. "I cannot accept."

"Please."

"No, it was a pleasure. The family of my wife has a ranch of many leagues on the Rio San Juan. They will be happy to see us and will provide us with new jobs and a new home. Please, do not insult me by offering money."

Pete stuck the pouch in his vest. "At least allow me to pay for the ferry."

The man nodded. When they shook hands, Tadeo pulled Pete close and whispered, "Watch yourself, *señor. Un Mal Hombre* will kill you if you are not careful. *Vaya con Dios.*"

As soon as they were safely across the river, Pete returned to the jacal. Buddy Pecos was already at work on the old Concord, replacing the rotting wood. The wheels, all needing new metal tires and three missing a handful of wooden spokes, were leaning against the corral. A fire roared in the pit in the front yard. Pecos would have his work cut out for him. So would Pete.

He looped a lariat over the Oldenburgs' necks, threw a war bag of grub and possibles over his saddle horn, and pulled himself onto his horse. Pecos looked up, wiped away sweat, and nodded, then returned to his carpentry. "I'll be back tomorrow night," Belissari said, "with the Americans. I want to see how Felipe and McBride are doing too. Watch yourself, pard."

"You too."

Buddy Pecos walked inside the shack late Monday morning, his clothes drenched in sweat despite the cold, face drained of color, eye burning red. He crashed heavily onto the chair and said, "Coffee, please."

Hannah shook her head. ''Buddy,'' she pleaded, ''you were at it all night. Get some sleep. You look a mess.''

The tall gunman shook his head. ''Can't,'' he said weakly. ''Still got them tires to do. Them kids ain't back yet?''

Pecos had sent Angelica and Paco to Ossian Philley's mercantile to pick up the metal rims for the stagecoach's wheels. The other children, and that stupid dog Obadiah, had gone with him, but he had only left five minutes ago.

''Buddy,'' Hannah said as she filled a tin cup with coffee, ''they just left.''

''Oh, yeah. Reckon I forgot.''

Hannah placed the cup in front of Buddy and stepped back, suddenly worried. Pecos's hands trembled, spilling half the coffee on the table. He managed to drink some, sighed heavily, and tried to stand, only to fall back into the chair.

She was at him in an instant, ordering him to rest, pressing the back of her hand against his forehead, then jerking it away.

''Buddy, you're burning up!''

''I'll be fine,'' he said. He tried to stand again, sat back down, weaved like a drunkard, and toppled hard onto the sod floor.

Chapter Sixteen

Malaria. The word struck Pete Belissari like the hind leg of a stallion. He sank wearily into the waiting bench at Burke's Barber Shop. Outside, he heard the rustling of a wagon's traces and an off-key piano playing in a cantina down the street. Hannah sat beside him, put her arm around his shoulder and gave a gentle squeeze.

"Now, laddie," Burke said, "it's not as bad as you think. Buddy Pecos has the constitution of a grizzly and says he caught the fever originally back in the War. More soldiers, Yanks and Rebs alike, died from fever than from bayonets and minié balls. Trust me. I was there. If malaria didn't kill him back then, I dare say it won't kill him now. But . . . he won't be driving a stagecoach anytime soon."

Pete dropped his hand from his face. "Can I see him?"

"Sure, if he's awake, but don't be too long. He needs rest."

He walked past the barber chair and into the back room, where Jarlath Burke performed his doctoring when he wasn't cutting hair or pulling teeth. Buddy Pecos lay on a narrow cot in the corner, sheets damp from his sweat, his one eye barely open. The dark eye patch and his many scars looked even more gruesome with his face now as white as sugar.

"Hey, pard," the old Rebel said weakly, "you finally gettin' your locks shorn?"

Belissari smiled and pulled up a chair beside the bed. He opened his mouth, couldn't think of anything to say, so he sat in silence until Pecos whispered, "I ain't gonna be much help to you."

"You never were," Pete joked, and Buddy tried to smile.

"You're gonna have to drive that stagecoach the whole trip," Pecos said. "Everhart can't help, not as busted up as he is. You'll need a shotgun rider, though. Know anyone?"

Pete shook his head. He tried to think of the men he could trust. Sergeant Major Cadwallader of Fort Davis? He was off on patrol. Julian Cale and Jack Leslie couldn't do it. He'd need Dave Goldman at Shafter Station. Chris? Too young. Irwin Sawyer? Not hardly. Besides, with the race running Wednesday, he'd be forced to choose someone in Presidio. The rules said that each stagecoach must make the full run with a driver, messenger, three passengers, and a strongbox. He looked at Pecos, but the ex-Confederate was asleep, so slowly he rose and quietly left the room.

"I'll ride with you," Hannah said.

"No."

They were back at the jacal where Pete had hired a man Dean Everhart knew to repair the wagon wheels. Belissari watched the man's every move, not that he knew anything about affixing metal tires to wooden wheels, but the fellow had done his job without any problems, taken his money, and left. It was Tuesday evening. The race was scheduled for tomorrow morning.

"Why not?" Hannah asked.

They were sitting inside eating supper. Dean Everhart was outside guarding the team of horses and refurbished Concord. The stagecoach operator was too banged up to put up a fight, but he argued that he could fire a warning shot if something happened, so Pete let him have Buddy's Schofield .45.

"It's too dangerous!"

Paco and Angelica barged inside with a ten-pound sack of apples, followed by Obadiah. Hannah started to shoo the dog outside, but relented. "Look!" Angelica shouted. "Look what that mercantile man, Mr. Philley, gave us!"

Hannah smiled. "I'll cut some up."

"He told us they're for our horses!" Paco interjected.

"That many apples will be enough for us and the horses," Hannah said.

"Can we cut 'em up?" Angelica asked. "We'll be careful."

"All right. Where are Bruce and Cynthia?"

"Outside," Angelica said. "Helping Mr. Everhart guard the stagecoach."

As the children found knives and began slicing up the apples, Hannah returned her cold stare to Pete.

"Dangerous?" she said, trying not to raise her voice in front of the orphans. "Everything we do out here is dangerous. You need someone to ride with you, and there's no one you trust. I drove a buckboard all the way from the ranch—with those kids and that dumb dog." She rolled her eyes. Paco was tossing chunks of apples to Obadiah, who was wagging his tail, catching the food in the air. She didn't know dogs ate apples.

''Look!'' Angelica yelled.

''Yes,'' Hannah said in surrender. ''That's nice.''

Hannah inhaled and exhaled. ''Petros,'' she said sharply, ''if you say something about it being a man's job, so help me I'll knock you out of your chair. Now who else is there?''

''Hannah,'' Pete began, but he quickly wilted. There was no one else. Not in Presidio anyway. ''All right, you ride on top. But only to your ranch. When we get there, I'll take one of those cowboys Julian Cale left you. Fair enough?''

She nodded. Belissari let out a breath. There was no rule that the shotgun rider had to make the entire trip. Coffey and Co. would probably spell its driver and messenger at each home station—the way it was supposed to work. And Pete was guessing that if Jill Coffey tried anything, it would be somewhere between Fort Davis and Fort Stockton, probably along that desolate run from Barrilla Springs to Fort Stockton where witnesses would be hard to come by. Hannah would be safe at the ranch by then, and Pete wouldn't mind sharing the front boot with one of Cale's riders. The rancher hired good cowboys who could ride and shoot—with the exception of Irwin Sawyer, of course.

Paco had become bored with feeding Obadiah and cutting up the apples, so he grabbed the half-full bag and said, ''Is it all right for me to go feed them horses, Pete?''

Belissari nodded and sipped coffee. ''Don't feed

them too much,'' he said, ''and let Bruce and Cynthia and Mr. Everhart have an apple too.''

The youth slung the sack over his shoulder and darted outside. Angelica carried the plate of sliced apples to the table. Obadiah was scratching on the door, so Angelica let him out and followed the pet around the house, leaving Hannah and the horseman inside to enjoy a moment of peace.

''I'm glad we didn't fight,'' Hannah said.

''Me too.'' He finished his coffee. ''Would you really have knocked me out of this chair?''

She smiled, her blue eyes gleaming, and replied, ''Yes, indeed.''

Hannah reached across the table and they locked hands. ''What are you going to name our new stagecoach?'' she asked. ''*Argo II*?''

Pete snickered. ''No,'' he answered. ''I was thinking about *Forlorn Hope*.'' Hannah laughed and released his hands, slowly rose and walked to him, then bent forward, her blond hair brushing against his unshaven face. Belissari closed her eyes, felt Hannah's lips upon his, then heard the door slam open and Angelica scream:

''Something's wrong with Obadiah!''

The dog lay on its side behind the shack, quivering and whimpering in the sand. Pete knelt beside it as Hannah held a lantern. Angelica, crying, dropped to her knees and brushed the mutt's head.

''He's going to be all right,'' she pleaded. ''Isn't he?''

Belissari leaned closer. Suddenly the dog vomited. Angelica cried harder, and Pete saw the pieces of apples. He shuddered, cursed and jumped to his feet, screaming as he raced around the *jacal* and to the corral:

"Paco! No!"

Dean Everhart had lit a fire in the pit. From the light, Pete saw Paco holding an apple and one of the horses nervously approaching him. The mare jumped back at Pete's shouts, but another horse, much bolder, inched its way toward the fruit. He screamed again, and Everhart must have realized what was happening because he stepped forward and knocked the apple out of the kid's hand, wincing at the pain that shot through his body. Paco yelled something, looking hurt, though not from Everhart's actions, and Cynthia and Bruce backed away as Belissari reached them. All three children looked frightened.

"But," Paco said with a whimper, "you said it was all right."

Belissari gathered the apples and put them in the bag. He wasn't sure of anything yet. It was just a guess. Hannah and Angelica hurried to the scene, where Angelica told them about Obadiah and all of the children sprinted around the house to the sick dog. Hannah went with the children, and Everhart followed Pete into the house.

Belissari tossed the sack on the table, then picked up one of the sliced apples. He smelled it first, bit off a piece and spit it out. Everhart stepped closer, taking a piece for himself. After spitting out his sample, he rinsed out his mouth with the leftover coffee in Hannah's cup and spit that onto the floor.

"Where?" Everhart said. "Where did those kids get these?"

"Ossian Philley," Pete replied.

"But why?" Everhart looked at the plate and shivered. "That's strychnine."

Belissari nodded, heard Hannah's call and slowly walked outside, around the shack and to the children, all of them crying, even Hannah, and she had never liked Obadiah. Pete knelt beside the dog again, rubbed its head, and looked into its pleading eyes. Pete felt the tears well and shuddered until he regained control. His right hand found the butt of his Colt, and he slowly drew the revolver.

"NO!" Paco shouted. "No, Obadiah will be all right! I promise!"

"Hannah," he said, "get these kids out of here."

"Please don't hurt Obadiah!" It was little Bruce, who rarely spoke. Cynthia and Angelica just bawled.

Belissari coughed once, sniffed, then bellowed, "Get them inside, Hannah! Now!"

"Come on," he heard her say, and he closed his eyes until the door closed. He thumbed back the hammer, pressed the barrel against Obadiah's head, and with his left hand, covered the dog's eyes.

The muffled gunshot unleashed a river of tears inside the jacal. She let Paco bury his face in her chest, and tried to hold all of the children.

"I . . . hate . . . him!" Angelica yelled between sobs. "Pete . . . killed . . . Obadiah."

"He didn't have to, did he, Mama Hannah?" Cynthia asked. "I mean, Obadiah could have gotten better."

Hannah shook her head, tried to stop her own tears from streaming down her face, but she couldn't. "Obadiah was sick," she said. "Really sick. And he was in a lot of pain. Pete had to do it, honey. And you don't really hate him."

"No," the girl said, dropping her head and wailing some more.

"It was them apples?" Bruce said, sniffling. "They were bad?"

Hannah nodded.

"I . . . I . . . I didn't know, Mama Hannah," Paco managed to say. "I promise I didn't know them apples was rotten."

"I know you didn't, honey," she said, pulling the seven-year-old tighter against her. "It wasn't your fault."

Pete entered without speaking. He found his battered hat, pulled it tight on his head, looked at Hannah and the crying children, then grabbed the sack of apples and slammed the door behind him.

Hannah pulled herself to her feet, wiping her eyes. "Children," she said softly, "I'm sorry. I'm sorry about everything. But I have to go."

Cynthia choked back tears, trying to be brave, and said, "We'll be all right."

"But I'm scared," Paco cried.

"I am too," Hannah said. She was frightened that someone in Presidio would risk poisoning her children to kill a team of horses to win a stupid stagecoach race, shocked at the rage that was boiling in her stomach. But what terrified her the most had been the look in Pete Belissari's eyes.

Chapter Seventeen

Ossian Philley fumbled with his keys, trying to lock the door to the mercantile. He dropped the metal ring onto the dust-covered boardwalk and cursed softly while picking it up; as he straightened Pete Belissari grabbed a handful of Philley's thinning, greasy hair and slammed his head against the door, shattering a glass pane.

Pete jerked open the door, shoved the mercantile owner inside, and slammed the door behind him, breaking another piece of glass. Philley staggered toward him, and Pete swung the sack of apples like a scythe, connecting solidly against the jaw, sending the sweaty little man sailing across the room, where he landed on a table and sent bolts of calico cotton bouncing across the floor. The poisoned fruit spilled onto the floor, and Pete tossed the empty sack aside.

The only light came from the street lamp in front of the hitching post, casting an eerie glow in the store. Belissari listened but heard only Philley's moans. The other stores along the street were closed, and Pete doubted if anyone would happen along down the business district anytime soon. He had Ossian Philley all to himself.

Philley gathered his hands and knees underneath him and mumbled something. Pete stepped forward and kicked. He felt the man's nose give way against his heel, saw him reel backward and crash hard in a sitting position against the long cabinet. Belissari jerked the coward to his feet, buried his fist in Philley's gut, and threw him over the desk. He leaped over it and pulled Philley up again, slamming his head against the brass cash register and then shoved him against the cabinet, where his flailing arms scattered pipes, tobacco, combs, and hair ornaments.

Belissari's left fist struck Philley in the mouth, then he grabbed the man's shirt front and jerked him forward. "You almost poisoned a bunch of kids!" Pete screamed in a voice he didn't recognize as his own.

Philley mumbled something incoherent and Pete slapped him savagely. "Who?" Pete shouted. "Who put you up to it, and why?"

The mercantile owner wailed something and wiped his bloody lips with the brown cotton sleeve stockings that protected his white shirt. "I . . . don't know what you're . . . talking about," Philley spit out.

Belissari slammed the palm of his right hand against Philley's throat, and the man collapsed at Pete's feet, gasping. When Philley could breathe again, Belissari lifted him and threw him across the room, knocking over two grinding mills and landing on top of a frame lever harrow. Pete walked forward slowly, pushing a corn and bean planter out of his way and squatting beside the sniffling man among the farm implements. Philley slowly rose off the light steel plow and collapsed on the floor, pulling himself into a ball like an infant.

"Who and why, Philley?"

The man mumbled something again, and Pete shot

up and kicked him several times, then crashed on top of him, pinning down his arms. Pete quickly drew the revolver, shoved the barrel against Philley's throat and thumbed back the hammer.

"I'm going to blow your head off," he said.

"Pete."

He looked up. He hadn't heard Hannah open the door, but there she stood, just a few feet in front of him, silhouetted by the streetlight. "Get out of here!" he snapped, but she shook her head.

"Don't," she said. "Don't do it, Pete."

He looked away from her. His eyes locked on Ossian Philley's terrified gaze. The Colt shook in his hand. In fact, Pete's whole body was shaking. Slowly Pete eased the hammer down and pulled the gun back a few inches, though it stayed pointed at the mercantile owner. Hannah let out a deep breath, found a lantern amid the wrecked store and fired it up. She gasped at Philley's bloody face.

"Tell me," Pete ordered.

"I . . . I . . ." Pete waited. The man cried a few minutes, then spilled it out: "I swear, Belissari, I told them kids not to eat them apples! I told them they were for the horses only! I never meant to hurt any kids."

"You didn't," Belissari said, "but you killed their dog."

Philley cried some more, then Pete pressed the gun barrel against his throat. "Why?"

The man sucked in a deep breath, whimpered, and bit his lip. Then he confessed: "I . . . I lost this place to Jill Coffey in a poker game. She was letting me run the business, but it was hers, kinda like she was my silent partner. I was just drawing a dollar a day. I . . ." He cried again, composed himself, and continued. "They told me if I did like they said, if I somehow got them horses poisoned, then I could get the deed back to this place. But I swear . . . I promise I didn't want anybody hurt. I . . . I just wanted—"

"Coffey!" Pete shouted. "Jill Coffey told you that?"

Philley shook his head. "Not her. But that shootist that's always with her. Tubac. And Cash Hardee."

Pete stood. "Philley," Hannah was saying, "we're going to take you to the town marshal. You're going to tell him everything you just told us."

"No!" Philley screamed. "No! They'll kill me. I can't do that. I can't testify against them. You don't know those men, what they're capable of! No. Please, ma'am. No! I can't. I won't!"

Pete cocked the gun and aimed at Philley's head. "Get out of here, Hannah," he said. "Now."

Hannah sprung in front of him, grabbing his right arm with both hands, forcing the Colt down, pushing Pete away. "No, Pete. Walk out of here. Walk out of here now! You don't know what you're doing." Somehow she managed to steer him toward the door. Belissari tried to turn around, tried to say something, but she pushed him against the wall. "Walk!" she said. "Walk outside! We're leaving."

He was still holding his revolver when he sat on the bench in front of a cobbler's store next to the mercantile. Hannah stood over him, biting her lower lip, forcing back tears. Pete angrily shoved the Colt into its holster, looked up, and snapped, "There's not a jury in Texas, in this country, that would convict me if I had killed Philley! I don't know why you're protecting him."

"It's not him I'm protecting," she said. "It's you."

He snorted, smiled without humor, and shook his head, which touched off her temper.

"You think you could live with yourself if you shot him down like that?" Her voice rose with each word. "In cold blood! That's not your way, Pete! And it sure isn't mine! You want to go back in there and murder him, go ahead. You've got the gun. I can't stop you. And then you can ride out of here and my life forever. Go on!"

His fists were clenched, the knuckles white. His body trembled. He shook his head and mumbled something. "No," he finally said. "I can't kill him. But I can kill Tubac and Hardee." Pete started to rise, but Hannah shoved him back onto the bench.

"No!" she yelled. "That's just what she wants. Hardee's probably at Fort Leaton waiting for you to try something. Tubac's with him. They'll kill you, and if you don't drive that stagecoach tomorrow we are finished. Is that what you want?"

"Then I'll take it up with Jill Coffey!"

"She's gone! Everhart said she went to Fort Davis this afternoon."

She knelt in front of him, taking his hands in her own, pleading. "Listen to me. This isn't the Pete I know. This isn't the Pete I love. I know you're angry. I know you're hurting. So am I, but we have to think about that race tomorrow, and those children. We'll make Philley testify. But after the race. The race has to come first. No, the race comes second. Paco, Cynthia, Bruce, Angelica, and Chris. They come first."

He spit out something that was part breath, part wail, part tears. Hannah crawled up on the bench beside him as he shuddered and cursed Obadiah. She brought her arm around his neck and pulled his head against her shoulder. He cried briefly, and she kissed his hair and hugged him. "I know," she whispered. "I liked that dog too. Everything will be all right, though."

He sat up and took a deep breath.

"Better?" she asked.

"Yeah," he said and apologized.

"You have a temper, Pete," she said. "You don't lose it often, but when you do . . ."

They were silent for a minute. Then Hannah said, "Pete, I want you to go back to the house now. This might be a ruse. Hardee and Tubac might try to run off those horses or steal the stagecoach, and Mr. Everhart is all alone. And I want you to bury Obadiah. Will you do that for me?"

He nodded. "What are you going to do?"

Hannah smiled. "I'm going to take a walk. I have a temper too, dear, and I need to cool down."

Slowly he rose, pushed his hat back, and left for the jacal. Hannah followed him for a while, making sure that he was going to the house, before she turned around and made a beeline for Diego's Cantina. She had lied to Pete. Jill Coffey was still in town.

She peered over the batwing doors, and through the smoke and crowd saw the gambler sitting at a table in the back, dealing cards to six men. Behind her stood a smiling Tubac, his thumbs hooked in his baggy jeans, leaning against the wall. Hannah pushed her way through the squeaky doors and ran into a man wearing the biggest white hat and biggest brown mustache she had ever seen.

"Hey, little lady," he said in a drunken slur, "this ain't no proper place for a—"

Hannah shoved past him and hurried to the card game, her fury rising. She stopped beside Coffey, controlled her breathing, and waited. Tubac's grin turned into a scowl, and the men at the table looked up from their cards and stared at her. Finally, Jill Coffey placed her cards on the green felt table and swung around in her chair, smiling pleasantly.

"Good evening, Miss Scott," she said. "Come to wish us luck for tomorrow?"

"It didn't work," Hannah said. She didn't like the way her voice sounded—too timid—so she lowered it an octave and repeated: "Your plan didn't work."

Jill Coffey cocked her head. "I don't know what you're talking about."

"Philley's apples didn't poison our horses," she said. "You did manage to kill our dog—and you broke my children's hearts and almost poisoned them."

"Orphans," Tubac corrected bitterly. "You ain't got no kids."

"Tubac," the gambler said, raising her right hand to silence him. Curiosity showed in Coffey's green eyes, which locked on Hannah. "I really don't know—"

Hannah bent over, placing both hands on the table near Coffey's cards and chips. Her voice was low and deliberate. "I've had it with you. So get this through your pretty little head: If you ever hurt *my children*"—

she glanced at Tubac, then stared at Jill—''again, I'll . . .''

She hesitated. Jill Coffey smiled. ''What? Kill me?'' she asked mockingly.

Hannah struck without thinking. Her fist caught Jill Coffey under her left eye and knocked her to the floor. Hannah stepped back, suddenly aware that the noisy saloon had gone silent except for the out-of-key player piano in the opposite corner, and she wished someone would turn that off. No one at the card table moved, although the men's jaws slackened. Jill Coffey was on her hands and knees, and Tubac jerked a shiny revolver from a dirty holster and aimed at Hannah's chest.

She braced herself, refusing to cower, and stared into the gunman's menacing eyes. Two of the men at the table started to rise and another gasped, but Tubac paid them no attention. Hannah figured she was going to die right here.

''Tubac! No!'' It was Jill Coffey's voice. The gambler pulled herself to her seat, rubbing the red spot on her cheek. ''Put it away,'' she ordered the gunman, and he complied, but he never looked away from Hannah. Coffey picked up her cards. ''Let's play poker, gentleman,'' she said calmly.

Hannah turned and walked out of the saloon.

Chapter Eighteen

Pete Belissari dipped the thin brush in the can of whitewash and painted the words ''Forlorn Hope'' on the underside of the driver's boot. He handed the can and brush to a smiling Paco, then slowly climbed aboard the battered Concord stagecoach, turned around, and helped Hannah aboard.

He had unbuckled his Colt and gun belt and left them in his valise with Dean Everhart. A short-barreled .45 wouldn't do him much good on a bouncing stagecoach—he had the twelve-gauge for protection—and Belissari didn't want to be saddled with any unnecessary weight.

They had paid off the jacal's landlord, and agreed on a plan. With Buddy Pecos still bedridden, they asked Burke, the barber-dentist-doc, if he would mind if they hired a bodyguard for their friend. It was a long shot that Hardee, Tubac, or one of Jill Coffey's other employees would try to hurt Pecos, but they didn't want to take any chances.

Jarlath Burke laughed at the proposition, reached behind his back and pulled out a giant Colt's Dragoon, a forty-year-old .44 that looked more like a club than a revolver.

''My dear friends,'' Burke said in his heavy brogue, ''if anyone tries to harm my patient, he'll find himself visiting St. Peter quicker than he can say 'Irish whiskey.' ''

Buddy Pecos, they decided, was quite safe.

After the stagecoaches left Presidio, Dean Everhart would file charges against Ossian Philley with the town marshal. Slaughter would probably leave town right after the two Concords, taking Tubac and Jill Coffey with him. With them and their corruption gone, Philley might feel a little more willing to talk. If not, he could rot in jail—providing he hadn't fled across the border. But Hannah doubted that. Philley wasn't going anywhere after the beating Pete had handed him.

Despite his injuries, Everhart had agreed to take the children back to Fort Davis in Hannah's buckboard. All except Cynthia. The nine-year-old had demanded to ride the stagecoach.

''Honey,'' Hannah had pleaded, ''it's not going to be any fun, bouncing around.''

''I have to go, Mama Hannah,'' she begged. ''I have to tell Chris and Irwin about Obadiah. I don't want them to hear it from somebody else. I have to go. Please.''

''But Cynthia—''

''I'll be good. I won't complain. But I just have to tell them. Obadiah was their dog too.''

Cynthia was almost crying now, and Hannah didn't have the heart to tell her no. The stagecoach would be in Fort Davis more than a full day before Everhart arrived. She glanced at Pete.

''She can get off at the ranch with you,'' he said, though she could tell by his voice that he didn't like the idea. ''I'll replace you and her with Cale's cowboys.''

So Cynthia swung open the door and found a seat inside. Paco and Angelica opened the gate, and the horses pulled the stagecoach out of the corral and to the bank, where the Coffey and Co.'s blue and black stagecoach sat parked and waiting. Hannah didn't recognize the driver or messenger. Both were hardened men, bearded, dirty, unsmiling.

Sheriff Slaughter and Judge McGrath stepped outside, smiling pleasantly over their morning coffee. McGrath read over the rules while a dark-skinned man in a canvas coat and plaid britches crawled aboard both stagecoaches, checking the strongboxes, making sure everything was in order.

"All right," Slaughter finally said. "You get three passengers—free of charge I might add—"

"We have one already," Hannah said.

Frowning, Slick Slaughter peered inside and stepped back, his scowl hardening. "A kid?"

"She wants to go."

The sheriff's gray mustache drooped some more. "A woman riding shotgun and a six-year-old for a passenger," he began, his anger obvious. "That's not fair. The weight—"

"She's nine," Hannah corrected.

"Whatever. But you must understand that we want to be fair."

Pete swore and mumbled something under his breath. Hannah fought back a smile. "There's no rules that say the messenger must be a man," Hannah argued. "And there's no rules that say a passenger must be a fat old man wearing a suit two sizes too small."

Slaughter's eyes burned as he sucked in his gut.

Judge McGrath guffawed. "She's right, Tyler," the judge said.

"All right," Slaughter said. "But to distribute the weight evenly, I'm picking your other two passengers."

"Fair enough," Hannah said.

Slaughter put two men in their stagecoach: a Mexican vaquero named Lozano who was on his way to visit relatives outside Fort Stockton, and a bearded, black-hatted man with a huge Winchester who said he was going coyote hunting for a rancher near Five-mile Mesa.

Inside the Coffey and Co. coach went a whiskey drummer clad in a sack suit and bowler, carrying his bag of samples. He probably weighed less than Cynthia, Hannah thought. A red-haired dressmaker on her way to visit her brother, who was a sergeant stationed at Fort Stockton, and a quiet, middle-aged schoolteacher in a calico dress climbed into the wagon after the drummer.

The man in the canvas coat threw the appropriate luggage in the rear boot of each stagecoach, pulled down the leather covers, and secured them with buckles and straps. He nodded at McGrath when he was finished and disappeared into the crowd.

Hannah glanced at the gathering of onlookers, maybe twenty or thirty men, women, and children. She looked for Jill Coffey, who was nowhere to be found. That relieved her. Not that she was ashamed of the scene she had made at the saloon, but she didn't want Pete to know she had lied to him.

"Where's Jill Coffey?" someone shouted, as if he had read her mind.

''Yeah, where's the Black Widow?''

''Miss Coffey and her bodyguard departed last night for Fort Davis,'' Slaughter answered. Hannah breathed easier. *Perfect.* Coffey must have left shortly after her run-in with Hannah.

''Well,'' McGrath said, ''I think things are finally in order. Any questions about the rules? Good.'' He nodded at Slaughter, who stepped between the two vehicles and drew his revolver.

''Gentlemen,'' McGrath said. He smiled, bowed at Hannah and added, ''And lady. May the better team win. Good luck to both of you!''

Slaughter's pistol barked. The Concord jerked, and Hannah gripped the bench with both hands.

The stagecoach bounded over the hilly, rocky terrain that some fools called a road between Presidio and Shafter. Pete Belissari lurched forward in the cramped driver's box and leaned back, holding three pairs of leather reins in his left hand and a long whip in his right. His red bandanna, which he had pulled up over his nose and mouth, fell, and he choked out a curse through the heavy dust and lashed out at the horses with the whip.

On his left sat Hannah, eyelids clamped shut, head facing down and to the side, both hands gripping the hard wooden seat so tight that her knuckles were white. She was supposed to be holding the shotgun, but had let the weapon drop into the coach's front boot. Pete couldn't blame her.

They had been on the road for just an hour, only another ten miles from their first swing station in Shafter, where Dave Goldman and Happy Jack McBride were waiting.

He put the whip aside and took a quick glance behind him. The pursuing Coffey and Co. stagecoach was maybe a hundred yards farther back, far off to his right. With the wind blowing southwest, he had a clear view of the competition and the two men in the driver's box.

Pete tried to tell himself that this was a marathon race, that it would be all right if Coffey and Co. took the lead early. But he couldn't convince himself. He had seen Coffey and Co.'s handiwork before, and if that coach got ahead of him, he wasn't sure what those men would do. He wouldn't put anything past them.

He was reaching for the whip again when a piece of the brake lever disappeared. Then he heard the second shot as a bullet zipped past his ear. Belissari turned, saw the white puff of smoke from a rifle and heard a bullet thud into the rear boot of his stagecoach. Coffey and Co.'s shotgun rider was shooting at them with a Winchester. This he hadn't expected—even from Jill Coffey.

Chapter Nineteen

Hannah Scott's eyes opened, and she looked at Pete in confusion. That confusion turned to shock, fright, maybe even anger, when Pete handed her the six heavy reins.

"Keep this coach moving!" he shouted.

"Pete! What are you doing?"

The team almost jerked her from her seat, but Hannah yelled and whipped the reins, then cringed as another bullet whined off a rock.

Belissari grabbed the Parker twelve-gauge but hesitated. The shooter was far out of shotgun range. His Colt was back with Dean Everhart—not that it would have done any good. He needed a rifle. Quickly he remembered that one of the passengers got on board carrying a big Winchester repeater. Belissari pounded the top of the coach with the shotgun butt and yelled, "Inside the coach! I need that Winchester!"

The man answered with a rifle shot. A piece of wood flew off the coach near the shotgun and Belissari reeled back, dropping the Parker and almost falling out of the boot and over the front of the stagecoach. He grasped the metal wires on the top of the Concord and pulled himself upright. Hannah looked on in horror.

That double-crossing passenger was working for Coffey and Co.

Another bullet knocked a bigger hole in the stagecoach. Hannah screamed and dropped to her knees inside the boot, though that wasn't much protection. Belissari looked up. Coffey's stagecoach was closing in. The stagecoach man fired again, and Belissari pulled himself out of the driver's box and onto the roof. He grabbed the shotgun and made his way toward the rear boot. Two quick explosions detonated from inside the coach. Two more holes punctured the roof inches from Pete's body, but Belissari moved on. Inside his stagecoach were Cynthia and that Mexican vaquero. He couldn't risk firing blindly into the coach, especially with a shotgun.

"Pete!" Hannah screamed again as a bullet clipped the strongbox near Belissari's feet. She yelled something else, something appropriate for a jehu—but Belissari didn't answer.

He looked at the pursuing coach, saw more smoke, heard the muzzle blast. Nothing sounded inside the coach. Belissari couldn't waste any more time. Rising on his knees at the rear of the coach, he swallowed, took a deep breath, and prayed that Hannah Scott wouldn't let the wheels hit a rock. Then, gripping the metal railing and his Parker double-barrel, he swung himself over the top of the coach and through the rear window just above the spinning wheel.

Belissari landed inside with a thud and a groan, bouncing against the rear seat and falling onto the floor, his legs in front of him on the middle bench, shotgun still in his grasp. A wide-eyed and gagged Cynthia sat on his left and the crumpled form of the vaquero lay at her feet. At the door in front of Belissari stood the third passenger, who was busy shoving cartridges into his Winchester. The man swore and was bringing around the rifle's muzzle toward Belissari, levering a fresh round into the chamber.

Ignoring the pain that rocked his entire body, Belissari raised the shotgun and pulled both triggers. Aiming was useless at this range anyway. His assailant disappeared in a thick cloud of acrid gunsmoke, but despite the ringing in his ears, Belissari heard the rifle clang against the bench. When the smoke cleared, the man with the Winchester was gone. So was the side door, and the rifle was bouncing its way out of the coach too.

Belissari dived and grabbed the barrel before the Winchester disappeared outside the Concord. He heard another bullet whine and knew the Coffey coach was getting closer, but first he took the gag out of Cynthia's mouth.

"You all right?" he asked.

"Yes, Pete," she said, though tears were already streaming down her face. "But I'm scared."

"Me too," he said. "But you have to help *Señor* Lozano. Then lie flat on the floor."

He was moving again, staring out the door opening. Not wanting to shoot from inside the coach, thus drawing return fire from the Coffey riders and risking injury to Cynthia, he shoved the Winchester on the Concord's roof and climbed back on top. The Coffey stagecoach was less than twenty yards away now. Belissari leaned flat on the roof, thumbed back the hammer of the Winchester, drew a bead on the Coffey shooter, and fired.

The rifle was heavy, an 1876 model in .50-95 caliber, and it kicked worse than Buddy Pecos's Sharps buffalo rifle. Belissari knew he had missed the second he pulled the trigger, but he jacked another round into the chamber and aimed again.

He saw the rifleman turn toward him. The man had fired his past two rounds at Belissari's horses, but now his attention was on the new threat. The .50-95 barked, the stock bruised Belissari's shoulders, and he missed once more. The rifleman fired. The bullet slammed into the strongbox. Hannah shouted and cursed. Belissari worked the Winchester's lever.

The Coffey rider fired first. Belissari felt a sudden burning across his right shoulder blade, warm blood running down his back. He ignored it, steadied the rifle as well as he could on a bouncing stagecoach, and pulled the trigger.

The rifleman was catapulted from his seat and over the back of the stagecoach. Meanwhile, the gunman's flying rifle barrel caught the Coffey driver across the throat. The jehu dropped the reins, pitched forward, and fell into the traces and under the wagon wheels.

Belissari turned his head. An awful way to die, he thought. Hannah was screaming at him, so he eased his way back to the driver's box and took the reins.

"Cynthia?" she asked.

"She's fine."

That settled, Hannah turned her wrath on Pete. "You idiot! Don't ever do something like that to me again! I can't drive a stagecoach!"

"You were doing a pretty good job," he said, smiling.

Hannah's expression went from anger to concern upon noticing the blood on his shoulder. "You're hurt," she said.

"A scratch. Doesn't hurt," he lied. The wound burned worse than Harry Troyer's Patent Horse Liniment.

He eased the six-horse team into a slower pace and sighed. The race was over before it had even begun. The Coffey and Co. Concord coach was running wild now. Ahead lay a rough road and deep canyon. Pete expected the runaway team to break its traces and send his competition's wagon into the abyss.

Suddenly he frowned. Above the creaks and groans of the stagecoaches, hard wind, pounding hooves, and snorting horses, he could make out a faint cry.

"Help!"

He swore, remembering that three passengers were also in the Coffey stagecoach—a whiskey drummer, a dressmaker, and a schoolteacher. *Had Coffey's men intended on murdering them too?* It didn't matter. If somebody didn't stop that runaway coach, those three people would be dead in minutes.

Pete shoved the reins back into Hannah's hands, then crawled back on the roof.

"What are you doing?" Hannah cried.

"Get us near the stagecoach," Pete said. "When it pulls alongside, I'll jump onto it and stop it. As soon as I jump, steer your team away from me and stop this coach."

"What?"

He didn't have time to explain. The Coffey coach was less than ten yards behind. "Move to the left!" Pete ordered, motioning with his hands. He steadied himself against the strongbox, knees bent, breathing suspended.

This was reckless, he knew. The two coaches could

collide, and then they could all be hurt, maybe even killed. But there was no other way to stop the runaway coach before it neared that broken canyon. Pete leaned forward as the Coffey coach paralleled his wagon. But just before he jumped, a wheel struck a large rock, knocking his coach off-balance and sending him crashing against the side of the Coffey and Co. Concord.

With both hands, Pete clung to the metal railing on the top of the Coffey stagecoach. His right moccasin brushed against the speeding front wheel, burning him, but his knees found the front windowsill and he caught his breath. Then two arms wrapped around his thighs and he heard a shrill voice: "Help us! Help us, please!"

Pete felt himself being pulled off the stage. "Lady!" he screamed, glancing at the spinning wheel, remembering how the Coffey driver had died. "Lady, you're gonna get me killed! Stop!"

He slipped again, but the grip on his thighs ceased. As he hung from the roof, he peered inside the coach and saw the schoolteacher and dressmaker dragging the panicking whiskey drummer from the window. Shaking his head, Pete made sure of his grip, pulled himself onto the roof, slid into the driver's box, and reached for the reins.

They were gone.

He saw them dangling against the traces and wagon tongue below. The canyon near Shafter was fast approaching, so Belissari reached for the brake lever and pulled it hard. The lever refused to budge. *This stage is as bad as ours!* he said to himself, forgetting that it once had been *ours,* and started to lower himself over the front of the coach and onto the tongue. It was the last thing he wanted to do: Inch forward to the lead team, then pull the horses to a stop. And he'd have to do it fast.

The wagon bounced again, spilling Belissari into the front boot where his head struck the toolbox. Bleeding slightly, Pete struggled to find his feet and stared ahead.

The horses had broken their traces and had sped off toward the right, sending the Coffey and Co. barreling toward the canyon's edge. Belissari recalled his Greek upbringing at that moment and said a *táma.* Then he slammed his fist on the top of the coach and screamed:

"Jump! Jump! Everybody out of the coach or we're all gonna die!"

The door flew open, and with a high-pitched yelp, the whiskey drummer leaped—or maybe he was thrown—out and bounced against the rocky road and disappeared in the dust. The dressmaker and schoolteacher quickly followed, and Belissari turned.

Too late. He leaped as the coach rolled over the edge, seemed to hang in midair for a lifetime, then dropped heavily among the broken boulders fifty feet below, crashing violently and leaving only twisted metal, splinters, and thick, white dust in its wake.

Chapter Twenty

She pulled back on the reins as hard as she could, groaning, pleading with the horses, and the stagecoach slowed and finally stopped. Hannah wrestled the brake and jumped from the driver's box. She watched in horror as the Coffey and Co. stagecoach broke loose from its team, the door swung open, and three figures jumped out. "Jump, Pete, jump," she mouthed silently.

The runaway Concord dropped into the canyon. Hannah closed her eyes as Pete left the stagecoach too late and fell with it.

She started walking, increasing her pace, toward the canyon rim. Behind her, Cynthia called out, but Hannah ignored her. Soon she was running, passing the schoolteacher, dressmaker, and drummer who had ridden in the Coffey coach. The thick dust from the wreck stopped her as if it were a wall. She didn't want to go farther, didn't dare look over the edge.

Wind carried the dust away. Hannah swallowed. There was nothing between her and the canyon's edge except brush and rocks. She took a tentative step forward, then saw a hand appear and grasp the trunk of a long-dead mesquite. Hannah couldn't move. Pete Belissari's head rose, then quickly disappeared along with his hand. His groan propelled her into action, and she sprinted to the edge just as his hand grabbed the mesquite trunk again.

Hannah dropped to the ground and gripped his hand with both of hers. She braced her boots against the mesquite and pulled, leaning back, every muscle straining and eyelids sealed shut. Pete yelled. Biting her lip, holding her breath, she kept at it. Her left foot slipped, and Pete's weight dragged her back a couple of feet before she managed to dig her heel into the dirt and stop. The rocks cut through her skirt, but she stretched back and wrestled with Pete, refusing to loosen her grip. When she opened her eyes, she saw him struggle and squirm and finally flop near her. They lay like that for what seemed hours.

He caught his breath, weakly managed to stand, looked at Hannah, and smiled.

His clothes were ripped and caked with dust. Blood flowed from his nose, head, and busted lips. His hair resembled a bird's nest, and his left arm hung limp at his side. Gone were his hat, bandanna, and right shirtsleeve.

"Lucky ledge," he said, nodding into the canyon.

"You're amazing," she said and had to laugh as she slowly rose.

"Pete!" Cynthia raced pass Hannah and wrapped her arms around the horseman, who groaned and pushed her back gently.

"Easy," he said. "I ain't in prime condition."

"*Ain't* ain't a real word," Cynthia said. "You never say *ain't.*"

He smiled and took her hand with his right. "Here," he said. "Help me back to the stagecoach."

"What's the matter with your left arm?"

"Broken. And some ribs."

Hannah untied the wild rag around her neck and gave it to Pete, who pressed it against his bleeding mouth and nose. They made their way to the other passengers. The schoolteacher and dressmaker were only scratched and bruised, but the drummer's left ankle was broken. The Mexican, Lozano, staggered forward and helped Hannah carry the whining drummer to the Concord, where they leaned against the stagecoach to rest.

Suddenly, the dressmaker began to cry. The schoolteacher went to comfort her, and the vaquero helped the drummer into the coach. Pete looked south, saw the bodies of the dead men. His stomach soured. "Folks," he said after a while, "we'll get you to Shafter Station. We'll report what happened. Then you can go on with us, or I'll get you an escort back to Presidio."

"You're continuing?" The drummer was dumbfounded. "After this?"

"We're a stagecoach company," Belissari replied. "You people that were on the Coffey coach, your luggage is in that wreck at the bottom of the canyon. I'll send someone for it once we get to Shafter. Now, I—"

A gunshot cut him off.

He looked up and saw about a dozen riders loping toward them. Mexicans by the looks of them. Except their leader. Belissari swore. *Cash Hardee!* A bullet dug into dirt thirty yards in front of them. One of the horses squealed, and the stagecoach squeaked.

"Everybody in the coach!" Pete yelled, biting back pain as he pulled himself into the front boot using his one good arm. Hannah crawled up beside him as he released the brake and grabbed the reins. Lozano handed Hannah the shotgun, then climbed into the coach where the door once was; Belissari flipped the reins, let go an oath, and felt the stagecoach lunge.

He screamed at the horses and told Hannah to check the Winchester. She bent down and pulled out the heavy rifle, ejected the spent brass casing, and frowned. "It's empty!" she yelled. Belissari swore again. Hannah dropped the rifle at her feet, reached across him, and found the whip. She snapped it, but the piece of rawhide jumped back and popped her chin. She tried again. Pete yelled at her to stop, but on her fourth try, the whip cracked above the leaders.

"Run!" she yelled. "Run, you horses!"

A bullet whined off the strongbox, too close for comfort.

Pete glanced at the pursuers. Hardee snapped a shot off with his Colt, though out of pistol range. Belissari wondered if the old scalphunter was acting on Jill Coffey's orders or just after revenge. Probably the latter, he thought. Maybe a little of both. Right now, the reason didn't matter.

Over the next few miles, the stagecoach distanced itself from Hardee's men. Pete's left arm throbbed. His throat and eyes burned, but after a while he could make out the outline of Shafter Station. He looked back. Hardee's men galloped, though they hadn't fired a shot in the past fifteen minutes. They were saving their horses and ammunition. Hannah cracked the whip.

"Put the whip down!" Pete yelled. "Pick up the shotgun and fire both rounds into the air!"

"What?"

He repeated his order. "To warn the station!" he added.

Hannah sat the whip behind her, found the Parker at her feet, and reloaded the weapon with shells from a canvas bag. She braced the stock against the bench, set both hammers, and pulled one of the two triggers. The shotgun boomed loudly, leaving a ringing in Pete's ears. A second blast quickly followed. Hannah tossed the shotgun back into the boot and reached for the whip. Pete could see movement in the station, horses dancing in the corral, men scurrying around like ants. He shouted at the horses and pounded the reins.

The stagecoach pulled into the dusty yard at Shafter Station and slid to a stop. Dave Goldman raced outside, holding an old Henry repeater. Happy followed him, groping his way along the crumbling adobe wall, a double-barrel Colt ten-gauge in his left hand. "Everyone inside!" Belissari shouted as he slammed the brake. Hannah was already on the ground, helping Cynthia down. Pete found the Parker, popped open the breech to eject the spent shells, and reloaded the shotgun.

He didn't expect Cash Hardee to attack the station—not this close to town—but on came the man and his riders, shooting now. Goldman returned fire, dropping to a knee, then picking his way to the corner of the building. Another shot rang from inside the burned-out adobe station, still serviceable with a canvas tarp for a roof. Lozano and Hannah carried the drummer inside, but the Mexican was outside in a second, brandishing a saddle ring carbine, and slammed the blackened door shut.

The riders were in the yard now. Bullets thumped the coach and adobe building. Horses screamed, and despite set brakes, the stagecoach inched forward two or three feet, pulled by the tired but frightened team. Pete looked up, saw Cash Hardee charging him on a magnificent black stallion. Belissari stood, thumbing back one hammer on the Parker as Hardee's horse slammed into the wagon like a locomotive. Belissari was flying through the air now. He heard the shotgun explode, though he no longer held the weapon, saw the stagecoach fall onto its side and the horses break away and gallop north—wagon tongue and all—then felt the air rush from his lungs, his broken arm and ribs searing with agony.

He lay on his back, dazed, but only momentarily. If he didn't move, he would die. Pete forced himself to breathe, looking first to his right, then left. The shotgun lay only a few feet away; he rolled over onto his broken arm, screaming from the pain, and shoved himself toward the weapon. His outstretched right hand grasped the walnut butt. He forced himself closer until his finger slipped into the trigger guard, and he tried to pull himself up.

Cash Hardee was upon him then, kicking Pete in the face with a black boot. Belissari yelled and fell back, releasing the shotgun. He tried to rise, but Hardee kicked him in his ribs, never letting up as they circled the overturned Concord. The punishment was brutal. He gasped, blinking away tears, vaguely aware of continuous gunshots, of people yelling in Spanish and English—but mostly shouts of rage and curses.

New gunfire erupted to the north. Some men from

Shafter had joined the fight, firing at Hardee's riders, giving Belissari newfound energy.

Pete kicked out weakly at Hardee and looked for another weapon, spitting blood and sand from his mouth. The scalphunter towered over him, Tiffany Colt in his right hand, curved knife in his left, pale eyes full of hatred. Belissari heard Hannah's scream, then he rolled over and tried to wrap his right arm around Hardee's legs, but the man only laughed and kicked Pete again in the head, a solid thump that turned Pete's world into a sea of blackness.

Hannah raced outside, oblivious to the bullets, and sailed into Hardee's back, grabbing his hair and jerking it savagely. The man dropped his knife, but kept his gun, laughing. She wrapped her right arm around his throat, reached out with her left and clawed the scalphunter's face. His laughter ceased. He backed up quickly and slammed Hannah into the stagecoach. She released her grip and fought for breath. Hardee's left hand slapped her hard. She slid down, vision blurred, as the man cocked his revolver and walked slowly toward Pete.

She sprang to her feet and leaped on his back again, digging her fingernails into his neck, biting his ear. Hardee swore vilely. They staggered back toward the stagecoach. Pete groaned. Then someone shouted. "Hannah! Get out of the way! Now!"

Hardee grabbed Hannah's arm and flipped her over his head. She somersaulted in midair and hit the ground beside Pete with a thud and a sharp cry of pain. The scalphunter spun around, jerked his revolver toward the voice, and pulled the trigger. A cannon—at least it sounded like a cannon—answered.

* * *

Pete Belissari swore and coughed. His eyes flittered, his vision cleared and he saw Hannah crawling toward him. "*¡Vamanos!*" someone shouted. "*¡El Diablo es muerto! Vamanos!*" More rapid words shot out, too hard to understand. Saddle leather creaked, and hooves pounded the ground. Hardee's riders were fleeing, galloping south as the gunfire diminished. Hannah lifted Pete's head into her lap and brushed the hair and dirt off his face. Despite her protests, he sat up, blinked, and looked at the overturned stagecoach.

Cash Hardee sat against the Concord, legs spread in front of him, dark blood pooling beneath him, rear wheel spinning over his head. The man tried to cock his revolver, still in his right hand, but he didn't have the strength. He coughed and said in the weak voice of a dying man: "You?"

Pete looked. Lozano and Dave Goldman stood in the yard, rifles at their sides, watching the fleeing bandits. But Hardee wasn't staring at them. His blue eyes were fixed on Happy Jack McBride, who was leaning against a charred cottonwood post on the cabin's porch, cradling a smoking shotgun.

Hardee coughed again. "You're supposed to be blind," he said.

"I am." Happy smiled. "But I hear real good."

The scalphunter swore, tried to lift the Colt again, cursed his weakness before surrendering, and looked at Pete and Hannah. His hate-filled stare returned to the blind old horse trader. Hardee sighed, and his chin dropped heavily against his blood-stained shirt, his wild eyes and sneer frozen in death.

Chapter Twenty-one

A huge crowd had gathered, cheering loudly, as the battered old Concord stagecoach pulled in front of Lempert's Addition in Fort Davis. Pete pulled on the brake lever, his face tightened in pain, and he slowly, unsteadily climbed down. Obviously, the telegraph lines were working, and word of what happened at Shafter Station had shot across the wires in Morse code.

Well-wishers and newspaper reporters swallowed Cynthia and the other passengers as soon as they were out of the stagecoach. Hannah dropped from the driver's box after Pete.

"Congratulations!" someone yelled.

"Y'all showed them!"

"Three cheers for Hannah Scott and Pete Belissari!"

Pete ignored them. He searched the faces for someone familiar and finally his eyes rested on the only one he really knew. He stepped forward and said, "Mr. Cale, loan me your Colt."

After glancing at Hannah, Julian Cale drew the revolver from his holster and offered it, butt forward. Belissari grabbed it with his good hand and shoved it in his waistband. That was a mistake. His ribs sent a spasm through his body, but he nodded his thanks at the rancher and slowly walked toward Lightner's Saloon.

"Pete!" Hannah ran and grabbed his right shoulder gently, but he kept moving. "Pete, you need to see a doctor. Let's go. This can wait."

"I've seen a doctor," he said. "And this can't wait." She let go, breathed deeply, and turned. "Cynthia!" she yelled. "Stay here." That had been unnecessary; the crowd and reporters weren't about to let Cynthia go anywhere just yet. Hannah took off after Pete, aware that Julian Cale and a few others had dropped in line behind her.

It wasn't really a doctor Pete had seen, but a miner had set his broken arm and manufactured a sling out of a bedsheet. The leftover cloth was used to wrap his ribs and minor gunshot wound across his shoulder blade. That would have to hold until he saw Captain Leslie. His right hand rested momentarily on the swinging doors at Lightner's. He saw her, sitting at a table and drinking wine as Langford Christlieb, the house gambler, dealt her five cards. Tubac sat beside her, guzzling whiskey from the bottle. They weren't gambling, just passing time.

Pete Belissari moved through the doors and went to her. Tubac rose, resting his right hand on his revolver, but Pete ignored him. The dark saloon had been empty. Apparently, most of the townspeople had been waiting for the arrival of the stagecoach. But a glance at the mirror behind the bar told a new story. Hannah, Cale, and a few others entered after Pete but kept their distance. Many other curious faces peered through the windows.

Without speaking, Langford Christlieb crushed out

his cigarette and took his place beside Robert the bartender behind the long mahogany bar.

Jill Coffey looked up and smiled. She wore the low-cut silk dress he had first seen her in, back in January when she had tossed him the poker chip and asked him to kiss it for luck, and new earrings. She ran her finger through a loose strand of auburn hair. Her eyes glittered.

"Congratulations," she said. "Looks like you have a mail contract. For now."

"Forever," Pete said. "You're finished."

"Help is hard to come by. I didn't tell those men to shoot at you. I'm glad you killed them. But as for being finished . . ." She laughed and sipped the red wine in front of her. "Oh, I think there are many hands to be played yet."

This sangfroid staggered him. He shot a glance at Tubac, then stared at the Black Widow. "It's over, Jill," he said. "Cash Hardee's dead. I'll make Ossian Philley and that renegade we captured back at Shafter talk—"

"I reckon you ain't heard." This came from Tubac. Pete turned to face the chinless gunman. The man smiled. "Seems like someone fed that Mexican rat poison in his coffee while he was sittin' in jail." Tubac's tiny head shook as he clucked his tongue. "Nasty way to die. And that Philley fella. He shot hisself in the head. Deader than a skunk."

"Tubac!" Jill gasped. She looked at the man as if she were surprised. Her hands flattened against the card table. Pete considered her for a minute, then looked again at the killer, whose smile turned into a laugh.

"You ain't got nothing, boy," Tubac said gleefully. "No witnesses, not that we done nothing. Nothing." He laughed again. Pete felt the blood rush to his head, his ears reddening, fury building. Jill Coffey had won. She was losing now, but Slick Slaughter would never throw her and Tubac in jail—not with Hardee's rider and Philley dead. She'd keep after him until she owned the stage line or was buried.

"Sure, you got the mail contract—once y'all get to Fort Stockton—but you gots only one stagecoach." Tubac was having fun now. "Something happens to that, Coffey and Co. is back in business." He looked at Hannah. "Something might even happen to your shotgun rider—"

A cry, not even human, roared from the pit of his gut, and his hand whipped out Julian Cale's long-barreled Colt. Tubac's smile vanished and he jerked his revolver, but Pete slammed the barrel and cylinder against the killer's head with a sickening thud, dropping him silently to the floor. Belissari backed away two steps, trained the barrel on Jill Coffey's head, and cocked the .45. Her green eyes were frozen with fear.

"Listen to me, Jill!" There was a lethal edge to his voice. "Your game is over. You're leaving town. Because if anything happens to any of my employees or that stagecoach outside—and I mean a stubbed toe or a broken spoke—I'll be visiting you. And if you think I'm bluffing, call my hand."

He pulled the trigger.

Hannah gasped. Jill Coffey flinched as the bullet destroyed one of her golden earrings. A tear rolled down her face, now drained a bloodless white. Pete Belissari turned sharply and left, handing Julian Cale his revolver and stepping outside into complete silence.

Poseidon snorted. Pete smiled and continued to comb the gray mustang's mane. With one arm in a sling, grooming his horses was about the only thing he could do on the ranch. He said softly, "I know. I've been ignoring you too long. But that'll change soon, boy."

"Stage is comin'!" someone shouted. He watched briefly as the Concord pulled into the yard and saw Chris, Irwin, and their hired hands begin changing teams. "Rear axle needs greasin'," the jehu barked before telling the passengers, "Folks, it'll be 'bout fifteen minutes. Stretch your limbs."

Pete's attention returned to his horse as he resumed combing. The voice chilled him:

"Mister, would you kiss my chip for luck? I'm having a bad run."

Belissari pushed himself away from the mustang and turned to face Jill Coffey. She wore a prairie dress of blue calico, flowered bonnet, and fine-lace shoes and carried a brown purse. It was the plainest outfit he had ever seen her in. Pete swallowed. Smiling, she flipped a poker chip toward him, but it dropped at his feet. He couldn't have caught it even if he wanted to; his left arm was in a sling, and his right held a curry comb.

Coffey stepped closer to him, admired Poseidon for a few seconds. Then she closed her eyes, took a deep breath, and held it for a while. Finally, she opened her green eyes, exhaled, and looked at Pete.

"I'm leaving town. Taking your stagecoach to Fort Stockton."

Belissari glanced at the other passengers, saw Hannah pouring them coffee. "Where's Tubac?" he asked.

"Dead." Jill frowned. "Sheriff Slaughter killed him the day before yesterday. Tubac . . . He . . ." She looked up, trying to find the words. "Ossian Philley was left-handed. He was found with a gun in his right hand, and someone in Presidio saw Tubac leaving the mercantile after hearing a shot. The marshal wired Slaughter. Tubac drew. Slaughter shot him with a shotgun."

Pete had no illusions that Slaughter was suddenly upholding the law. By killing Tubac, Slick had been protecting himself, keeping his name from being tarnished in a courtroom trial. But Belissari kept those thoughts to himself.

A full minute passed. Jill blinked away a tear. She sniffed, but refused to cry.

"I made a mess of things."

Pete waited.

"Pete," she blurted, "Pete, I never told Tubac to . . . I mean, I told him to make things rough for you. The fight at Barrilla Springs. Stuff like that. That was my idea. But I didn't want anyone hurt badly—and I never knew he killed poor old Philley or Hardee's man. And those poisoned apples. That was all Hardee and Tubac." She wiped her face with a hanky.

"Do you believe me?"

Honestly, he didn't know if he believed her or not. But he said he did, and Jill forced a smile. She shot a glance behind her. "I've got to go," she said, but stepped closer, reached into the purse, and withdrew a thick envelope. "Here," she offered.

Pete tossed the curry comb aside and took the package. Because of his broken arm, he had to place the envelope on a fence post to open the it. He looked inside, amazed at the wad of greenbacks, a check for five hundred dollars payable to bearer, a few other banknotes, and gold coin.

"That's all I have," she explained, "after selling off the livestock, paying everyone. It's all my winnings. I want you and the others to have it. It's the least I can do. I owe you."

He stared at her. "Where are you going?"

Jill shrugged. "Fort Worth to begin with. I can get credit at the White Elephant Saloon. I'll set up a game there, maybe win enough money for a train ticket."

"To San Francisco?"

She shook her head. "Home, Pete. I'm giving up on San Francisco. I still have a mother. In Vermont. If she'll see me."

The jehu shouted, "Back in the coach, folks! 'Bout time to ride!"

Pete looked at the envelope. He thought for a second, then awkwardly pulled a couple hundred dollars out and shoved them into his pocket. That, he figured, would help pay the medical bills for Felipe, Happy, Pecos and himself, help repair Shafter Station, and maybe cover a few other incidental expenses. He handed the rest back to Jill. There was probably close to two thousand dollars remaining.

"Take it," he said. "Besides, I owe you for an earring."

She laughed and touched her right earlobe. But her smile turned sad. "Pete," she said, "I can't."

"Take it. And do this: When you get to Fort Worth, don't go to the White Elephant. Go to the train station and buy a ticket to New England."

"For you?" There was a twinkle in her eye.

"For you. Go home, Jill. Leave the Black Widow for the dime novelists."

She looked away. "It's too late for me."

"It's never too late."

"All Aboard!"

She took the envelope, returning the money to her purse, then staring at Pete again. "I thought 'all aboard' was for trains." Belissari shrugged. "You really are special, Petros Belissari," Jill Coffey said. Her hand brushed a lock of hair from his face and lingered on his cut and bruised forehead. She rose on tiptoes and softly kissed his lips. "God bless you," she said, turned quickly, and ran to the stagecoach.

She ran straight past Hannah Scott.

Hannah said nothing. She just stared at Pete. His arm started hurting again, along with his ribs and head. The jehu shouted and cracked his whip, and the old Concord rolled out of the yard and toward Wild Rose Pass.

"Um," Pete began. "I . . . uh . . . she . . ."

The children yelled and ran into the corral. Chris and Angelica struggled with a wooden crate, which they dropped at Hannah's feet. All five kids grinned excitedly. "Look!" Paco shouted. "Look, Mama Hannah. Look, Pete. Look what she gave us."

Pete stepped forward and saw the furry little puppy

in the box. Paco jerked the dog up and thrust it in Pete's face.

"Easy!" Cynthia said. "Don't hurt it."

"Jill Coffey gave it to us." Paco's words ran together. "The Black Widow. She gave it to me. To us. Do you think we can name it Obadiah too?"

Pete petted the dog and gently placed it back in the crate. It was a collie, he thought, maybe twelve weeks old. He smiled at Paco. "I don't think," he said, "she'd like that name."

"You mean it's a girl dog?" Angelica asked.

Pete nodded.

"A *girl* dog!" Paco sounded thoroughly disgusted, but he looked at the whimpering puppy and smiled. "That's all right. She's a pretty dog."

"Can we feed her some milk, Mama Hannah?" This came from Cynthia.

"Please," Bruce begged.

Hannah nodded. She couldn't help but smile.

Chris handed Pete an envelope. "Miss Coffey said to give this to you," the teen said. Pete took the envelope and looked inside. The check and most of the money were still there, but some of the cash was gone. Maybe, he hoped, enough to buy a train ticket from Fort Worth to Vermont.

"Let's go!" Paco ordered, looking at the puppy. "She might be thirsty!"

Bruce and Chris lifted the crate and hurried to the cabin, followed by the two girls. Paco glanced at the stagecoach, now disappearing behind the mountain pass, and said, "I reckon Jill Coffey isn't all bad. You think?"

Belissari raked the kid's hair. "No," he answered. "I reckon she's not all bad."

Then Paco was screaming at the other orphans to wait for him, leaving Pete alone with a silent Hannah Scott.

She stared at him again. Pete straightened. "That kiss . . . uh . . . well . . . I . . ."

"I know." Hannah smiled. "I heard everything."

His pains died down. He was relieved, though a little perplexed. "You're not mad?"

Hannah shook her head. "Oh, I wouldn't make a habit of letting beautiful women kiss you, but . . ." She hesitated and stepped closer to him, brushed that disobedient strand of dark hair from his eyes. "That was sweet of you," she said. "What you told her. She's right: You really are special."

Her fingers brushed his face, smoothed his mustache, touched his lips, and slid along his neck and into his long hair.

"In fact," she whispered, "I just might kiss you myself."